'I promised you a demonstration of how we treat traitors,' El Fiero said. 'A man whom we placed in a hacienda farther north told of our plans. Diego! Fetch him.'

One of the half-breeds bowed and disappeared. El Fiero took the whip and weighed it in his hand. 'A sabadilla,' he said, 'is nine and a half foot long, weighs four pounds, and has a tail of three plaited strips studded with silver pieces. I have found that it is most effective . . .'

As a half-naked man was dragged in and chained to the wall El Fiero said, 'I would like your full attention now, Mr Kane. Twenty lashes should be enough. It usually is. Would you mind counting—loudly?'

Also by Louis Masterson

WITHOUT MERCY
THE CLAW OF THE DRAGON
THE STAR AND THE GUN
BACKED BY THE LAW
A RANGER'S HONOUR
MARSHAL AND MURDERER
PISTOLERO
THE MONSTER FROM YUMA
THE DEVIL'S MARSHAL
GUNSMAN'S INHERITANCE
REVENGE
STORM OVER SONORA
THE LAW OF THE JUNGLE
NO TEARS FOR MORGAN KANE
BETWEEN LIFE AND DEATH
RETURN TO ACTION
RIO GRANDE
BRAVADO
THE GALLOWS EXPRESS

and published by Corgi Books

Ransom

Louis Masterson

CORGI BOOKS
A DIVISION OF TRANSWORLD PUBLISHERS LTD
A NATIONAL GENERAL COMPANY

RANSOM

A CORGI BOOK 0 552 09247 9

First publication in Great Britain

PRINTING HISTORY
Corgi edition published 1973

Translated from the Norwegian by Phil Newth

This book is set in Georgian 10/11 pt.

Corgi Books are published by Transworld Publishers Ltd.,
Cavendish House, 57–59 Uxbridge Road, Ealing,
London, W.5.

Made and printed in Great Britain by
Richard Clay (The Chaucer Press), Ltd., Bungay, Suffolk.

NOTE: The Australian price appearing on the back cover is the recommended retail price

RANSOM

CHAPTER ONE

They call it Sabadilla—a whip of plaited rawhide and hemp. It's about eight feet long. At the far end it has usually sharply honed small triangles of iron or balls of lead. There are Mexicans who can tear out an eye with one crack of the whip, without touching the eyebrow.

The whip was banned for about ten years after the American Civil War. The government didn't like the idea that a large portion of the general public was being disfigured for life and often crippled by the Sabadilla. It was, generally, used as a weapon.

In the 1880s the whip had almost been forgotten. The younger generation had learned to use other weapons—guns. But the Sabadilla was still used at some places. The Rurales—the feared, despised, brutal government troops used them. Mexico's secret police used them.

And it was used in the Sonora State Prison, the feared Casa Fronteras, the dark, horrible stone Moorish-styled fortress that the Spanish had built a couple of hundred years earlier.

Casa Fronteras was surrounded by an eighteen-foot high wall made of chunks of roughly hewn stone. Inside the prison were dark, threatening stone cells with their small, barred windows. Along the top of the walls the apertures for firing through glared down over the landscape, a reminder of the merciless Spanish justice and their fear of a revolt among the poor Mexicans.

Casa Fronteras stood on a low hill, a mesa of hard, volcanic rock. The slope up to the walls was a mass of pebbles and weathered chalk stone. Two roads wound their way up to the door in the wall. The old moat and drawbridge had been unused and rotting for years. The iron-studded oak door in the wall was so solid that a stick or two of dynamite was the only thing that would bring it down. This was the only door in the wall. The guards in the watch towers on each side of the gate had a clear view over the road and gate and over the large square between the buildings in the fortress itself.

The low administration buildings, the cells and the walls themselves were built of stone. They stood on solid rock. About forty feet down in the ground rock, the Spanish had blown out huge rooms for their ammunition and supplies. When the government took it over as a prison these rooms were made larger into underground galleries that contained seventy single cells. These cells were eight feet high and six feet square. There were no windows, just a small aperture in the iron door. It was opened three times during the day—when the prisoners were given food.

Thirty-eight prisoners serving life sentences sat in these holes. Some had been there for years. The oldest one—who still hadn't lost his mind—had been there for twelve years. Twelve years in the darkness, in his own excrement, without seeing light except that which shone through the aperture or the short hours of exercise in the yard.

All together there were two hundred and twelve prisoners in Casa Fronteras and roughly a hundred guards ... a meaningless sum, compared with other prisons in the country. But there was a reason for it. The prisoners in Casa Fronteras were the worst criminals in society—murderers, rapists, arsonists, terrorists and robbers. Not one of them was serving a sentence of less than twenty years.

The guards in Casa Fronteras were known for their sadistic methods of treatment. Numerous tales were told in Sonora of the terrifying punishments that were dealt out to the convicts who broke the regulations. Up to six days in the ice-cold water in underground wells, weeks in a small shaft where the convict had to stand in an upright position and could only just breathe, punishment exercise with heavy, iron balls chained to the ankles—and then the worst of all—the SABADILLA! Chained to a wall naked—while the whip sang and the screams echoed between the dark walls...

It was natural that people stayed as far away as possible from the threatening fort. Travellers often took a roundabout route to avoid the place. Poor shepherds that dared to glance at the apertures for the cannons crossed themselves quickly and hurried away with their flocks.

Casa Fronteras was a symbol of everything that was wicked, evil and threatening.

In cell number 24 a man sat alone in the darkness. If there had been light in the cell it would have shown that he was white—an American. He sat on the short bench with his blankets around him. He had learned to put up with the cold after eleven months. His body refused to die. Pneumonia hadn't killed him—as he had hoped it would. The stinking remains of food that were thrown in three times a day through the hatch contained exactly enough nutrition to prevent one starving to death. His stomach had grown accustomed to the food and greedily spared every bit of nutrition possible. He had taught himself to eat without paying attention to taste or smell. He had a feeling in his hands that often amazed him. His eyes and ears were like an animal's. Through the cracks around the iron plate in the hatch he could make out almost invisible shadows when the guards walked past with oil lamps which were hung at certain distances down the gallery. His ears picked up the sound of footsteps at a great distance and he knew immediately which of the guards were coming—or going. Through the massive stonc walls he picked up sounds that none of the guards would ever hear. Every sound told him something. He had learned the underground language which was beaten on the walls with a piece of bone.

He didn't wish to die any longer now. He was a link in the silent, underground army—he listened to and spoke the same language as his fellow convicts. He was no longer alone. He wanted to stay alive.

He was called Clay Sanderson, was twenty-four years old and was in Casa Fronteras for life—for murder. He had gone berserk in a village south of Montezuma and had killed four Mexicans in a fight. He was sure the Rurales had spared him purposely. A bullet was too easy for a loco American.

The case against him was brief. It took the jury four minutes to find him guilty and the judge ten seconds to sentence him to life in Casa Fronteras.

Even now—after eleven months—he remembered the day he had been driven through the gate after the meandering road had ended. He remembered the grinning guards, the hot sun, the warmth from the walls, the dust, the taste of defeat in his mouth.

He remembered the wall with its two iron bolts, he remembered the sound of his clothes being torn off, the clatter of the chains as he was hung up on the bolts and the sound of the whip as the guards tried the whip by cracking it in the air.

Clay Sanderson was given twenty lashes with the Sabadilla and only his steel-hard will-power and stubborn fitness helped him survive.

Later he was told that lifers, prisoners in for a life sentence, were given a good thrashing with the whip—as if to scar them for ever. And all whites were beaten—no matter what their sentence was. Most of them died, their sores turning poisonous and their muffled screams telling the other inmates that another convict was struggling against death again.

At first he had no feeling of time. Life was one, painful night. But his body slowly got used to it, his determination to live slowly grew again in the dark cell and then came the day when he heard the sounds coming through the walls—muffled sounds of life. In the short hours spent in the exercise yard he learned the basic rules of the language—one of them was to talk, talk out of the corner of the mouth, a convicts' way of talking. Every third day the convicts were herded together in the yard, a hot, dusty, hundred square yards of ground. Sanderson could soon talk with some of the prisoners. And with a shock he realised that he would soon look the same way as they did.

Just two months ago he heard rumours.

Someone had managed to escape.

He didn't know who—or which. They all looked alike, with ragged hair and beards, as skinny as skeletons, filthy and hollow-eyed as skulls.

Later the underground 'grapevine' confirmed these rumours, three of the convicts—three WHITE convicts—had vanished.

Nobody knew how they had managed to get away. Casa Fronteras was supposedly escape-proof.

After a while more escaped. A couple of Mexicans. A white man. A half-breed. Nobody knew what happened to them.

One day a face had vanished.

No alarm was sounded. They never heard shots or the howling of the horrible guard-dogs—huge mastiffs—that ran around loose at night.

One day a face was missing in the exercise yard...

Sanderson wondered if they had been removed in silence—and executed. Maybe the sentence had been carried out after being changed. Maybe the warden had sent for them. Maybe he was a sadist who had to kill a person every full moon. The prisoners discussed it seriously. Nothing was TOO incredible in Casa Fronteras.

Or maybe they had taken their own lives in their cells. Or died quickly, naturally. Maybe they had been removed and buried in silence.

Clay Sanderson sat with his head bowed in the darkness. He drew the blanket closer around him. The stench of mould from the walls went unnoticed. He waited for the hours when the walls became alive again.

His ears heard footsteps.

He stiffened. Four men came down the gallery. Why?

The last round after supper had gone past hours ago.

The footsteps came nearer and nearer. Muffled sounds came from the walls. Other convicts had heard the footsteps. They asked each other what was happening.

Sanderson didn't answer, even though he could have told them the answer.

The guards stopped by his door. A light flickered in the hatchway, then the bolt was drawn back.

Sanderson raised both hands to his eyes. The light burned like fire in his eyes.

'Sanderson?'

'Yes.'

He squinted towards the doorway, breathed in the damp, cellar-like air and stared at the four guards.

'Come here.'

Sanderson was suddenly terribly afraid. What did they want with him? Kill him? Torture him? Was it the full moon tonight?

The cell suddenly seemed very safe.

'Wha ... what is it?'

They grabbed him and dragged him out.

'Shut up Sanderson ... or else ...!'

The door to cell 24 was locked again. The footsteps vanished down the gallery.

Through the walls the message ran quickly:

A prisoner has been fetched!

They knew another face would be missing in the yard next day ...

CHAPTER TWO

Morgan Kane was drunk—and was well aware of it.

He let his horse jog northwards along the dusty, broad track from Kansas City to Fort Leavenworth, deciding its own speed. It had been a short adventure and he was glad it was over. It hadn't done any of them any good and they separated without hard feelings or bitterness. Kane knew that after he had started to wear the U.S. marshal star again women had started to play a domineering role in the periods between assignments. Why did he ride into town so often? Why did he walk the streets, without aim or reason, staring at them from under the brim of his hat? What was he searching for?

Deep in his subconscious mind a picture had formed, getting clearer after a while—and now it hurt his eyes. It was a picture of that windswept, naked rise in the little valley over in New Mexico, where bushes clung to the hillside and a cross leaned against the north wind. Was the cross still standing? Or had wind and weather and time destroyed it—removed the last memory of Linda and the only happy time in his life; the only episode that had meant so much that it had changed him as a person?

Because it had only been an episode. Short—so terribly short.

Kane lit his cigarette. He could make out the lights from the camp far away. The movement of the horse rocked him into a strange, conscious doze. His body was heavy, lame, feelingless, but his brain was crystal clear-alive, so damned alive!

The brain coldly analysed the man who sat on the horse under the blazing sun; the lean, scarred, hard man with the bitter, brutal mouth and the rubber band on his right hand that after a while had become his trade mark. The hand with the band and the scar was a part of him, just as the service revolver and the tense nerves that by sight and sound registered everything that moved or made a sound around him. The brain classified him as a man with an inborn restlessness, a man without roots, an individual cut off from the rest of the flock—a lone wolf. His brain told him that the woman in Kansas City had seen through him, had seen inside his cold, empty interior. SHE hadn't known that it had been cold a long time—ever since Linda died. He had never found anything to fill the emptiness. He did his job, kept his fighting strength up to scratch and didn't notice that as work and time passed it had made a new person of him—a killer who hid a weakness that perhaps wasn't there at all. Weakness was his worst enemy. He wore a state marshal's star. In his work weakness was worse than being crippled. It meant death.

Was he searching for a new Linda? Was he trying to change again for the second time? Was his mind trying to do that? HIS MIND? What was that? The equipment that thought? Senses that warned their needs? That gnawing, whispering conscience? WAS THAT HIS SOUL?

The silhouette of the fort appeared—the long buildings with their lines of illuminated windows, the mess halls, stables, offices and workshops.

This was his home.

The guard appeared in the gateway.

'Kane?'

'Yeah,' he answered, grumpily.

'Shane wants to talk to you—and fast.'

Kane swore. The guard heard him. 'Got a belly-full?' he snapped.

Kane grunted in reply.

'Got a coffee pot on the go,' the guard went on. 'Empty that and get your head under some cold water.'

Kane did as he said and felt clearer in the head as he tramped across the dark square towards the well-lit admin. building. The adjutant sniffed with distaste when Kane asked him to warn Shane.

Some minutes later he stood in front of the small, slim man behind the writing desk. Shane was pale. His eyes—that were usually as clear as crystal—were bloodshot. He smiled, pale and drawn.

'Sit down, Morgan. Looks as if you need to.'

Kane sank into a chair. 'Thank you, sir.'

'Sorry to disturb you.'

'That's okay.' Kane tried to look interested. But a throbbing pain nagged at the back of his head. It grew steadily worse.

Shane pushed a yellowed, shining document across the table.

'This has been sent from the governor's office,' he said dryly. 'It was sent by the chief of police in Chihuahua, Mexico.'

Kane was suddenly all ears.

'If we knock off ninety per cent of "honoured senor" and "I have the great pleasure" and other niceties we're left with a short and honest guestion; "Do we know of a gang in West Texas that have specialised in kidnapping daughters of rich Mexicans for ransom?" The answer is "NO". I've contacted the Ranger Corps and the marshals concerned. If it hadn't been for these two things'—Shane waved them in the air—'I would have answered "no" in a letter of about a hundred words... But these are very interesting, they're from the local "*comisaire de policia*" in Chihuahua and briefly tell the following facts. Two months ago the daughter of a certain Don Luis Alvarado was kidnapped from her father's hacienda by a gang of unknown men. Three weeks later the daughter of a "grande" in Aquiles was taken away in broad daylight. Two vaqueros that were escorting her were killed. A vaquero was killed during the first incident too. One of the kidnappers was killed during the fight. HE WAS WHITE.'

Kane was squinting. His headache was killing him.

'Oh yeah,' he said. It sounded stupid and meaningless. He clenched his teeth.

'Near Aquiles a white man was found, killed by gunshots with a bag of gold pesos in his pocket. We presume that he was one of the kidnappers from Aquiles. That means a white kidnapper in each incident.'

'That's no proof that it's the same gang,' Kane said, hoarsely.

'The Mexicans checked them thoroughly before burying them, Morgan,' Shane said. 'Both men had the same marks.'

'Marks?' Kane spat out the question.

'Yes. Both bore the same marks on their backs, the marks or scars from a terrible beating with a whip. The rumour about these men spread over the whole of east Mexico like a prairie fire. The Mexicans have put a name on them.'

Shane met Kane's eyes.

'FLAGELLADOS . . . THE WHIPPED ONES.'

After a while Shane went on, 'The chief of police in Chihuahua has no clues. But he presumes—and maybe he's right—that since these men are white there's a good chance that they're staying on this side of the Rio Grande.'

Shane got up and went over to a wall map. He put his finger on the western corner of Texas. 'Zachary is down in El Paso. He says in his report that during the last three weeks four gunmen with guns to hire have headed towards the border.'

So that's where Ed was heading for, Kane thought.

'Zachary thinks that they'll sell their guns to worried parents in Chihuahua who feel threatened. The Police chief is also aware of this traffic. He's not pleased about it. He thinks these guns will cause more trouble than they'll prevent.'

Shane nodded to the map again. 'You know your way around these parts,' he said quietly, 'and you talk fluent Spanish. Any special reason that you won't take the job?'

Kane noticed a harder note in Shane's voice. Was he starting to draw in Kane's reins? Or was there a growing discord slowly developing between them? Kane moved uncomfortably in his chair. Something similar had pushed him slowly out of the Ranger Corps, the quarrel between the cold, calculating Major Monroe and his jealous, sly, second-in-command. Kane watched Shane carefully, trying to read his thoughts.

'You've had a tough time lately,' Shane said calmly. 'If you want to slide out of this job, I'll understand. Vernon can take it.'

Kane suddenly felt relieved. He almost smiled but stopped himself.

'I'm okay,' he said. 'It's pleasant in Chihuahua so early in the spring. I'll leave whenever you like.'

'Thanks.' Shane waved at the map with his cigar. 'As I said, Ed Zachary is in El Paso. He started investigations about three weeks ago, but we won't get any further until we've put another man—that means you—right now, into the country. We've nothing concrete to go on, no clues, no contacts. You'll just have to use your instinct. The Ranger stations and the local marshals are at your disposal—we've telegraphed instructions about you and Ed. Apart from that the police chiefs in Ciudad Juarez, Aquiles and Piedras Negras have been asked to give you full support.'

He saw Kane's almost unnoticeable shudder and grimace. 'I know,' he said, dryly. 'The big drum is being beaten! Everybody knows about it. But the governor's getting it from the top. He's terrified about any further border incidents. These reports will keep the authorities in Chihuahua calm. On the surface it'll look as if we're all activity.' Shane smiled quickly. 'But only you and Ed are working on the case. You in the field—to coin a phrase—and Zachary to back you up and be your contact between you and the ranger stations and the Mexican authorities. I'd like you to leave tomorrow morning, early, if that's okay by you?'

'Any time, sir.'

'Good! The quartermaster has money and tickets for you. Good luck, Morgan.'

Kane took the hard hand. 'Thanks,' he answered, briefly.

CHAPTER THREE

Four days later Kane jumped down on to the platform at El Paso. He felt exhausted and dirty after the long, boring train trip. He had played poker continually with a couple of cattle buyers and by a fantastic stroke of luck had won almost two thousand dollars.

He threw his bag across his shoulder and trudged over to the station building. It was late in the day and the glowing west-Texas sun still burned strongly in the hazy sky. He tried to keep to the shadow as he turned the corner of the station building and crossed the main street. He wondered which hotel to choose. The Cattlemen's Hotel was tempting but for some reason or another he chose the El Paso Hotel a little farther up the street. He wouldn't look for Zachary, as Zachary was most likely watching him and would make contact later.

Kane asked for a room at the rear of the hotel. A grey-haired fat man in a large-checked shirt and fantastic whiskers checked the guest book.

'Room twenty on the third floor, sir. That suitable? Sign in here, please.'

Kane checked in under his own name.

The man turned the book. 'Mr Kane, how long will we have the pleasure of your staying with us?'

'No idea.'

A quick smile. 'Makes no difference, sir. Can we get something for you . . . something to freshen you up?'

'Water for a bath and a bottle of Bourbon. Harper's preferably. And a jug of water.'

'I'll fix it, Mr Kane. One moment, shall I take your baggage, sir?'

'I'll manage it myself.' He lifted the heavy bag and went up the stairs.

An hour later the bath water had been removed and Kane sat in front of the open window, stripped to the waist, sipping his drink. It was very quiet outside. That's because of the heat, Kane thought. People stayed indoors. From the window he looked down into a dusty back-yard. There was shade there and the slight puff of wind was almost cool.

When someone knocked on the door Kane automatically whipped out his ·45 Colt 'Police' Special. He sat with it in his lap as he shouted, 'Come in.'

Zachary stuck his head in.

'Howdy, Morgan!'

'Hi, Ed. Come on in and get yourself a drink.' Kane threw his gun over on to the bed. Zachary pulled off his dark jacket and threw it after the gun. He sat opposite Kane and poured himself a drink.

Kane said, 'I presume you know this business with the El Flagellados better than I do. Shane could only give me reports from Mexico.'

'I don't know much more myself. Two days ago a guy came into town—the sheriff gave me the nod so's I could give him the once-over. He's called Babe Lago, a guy from Nueces. Down there he was known as the fastest gun since Buck Duane and young Hardin's days ... a man that could put three into the ace of spades. He's not wanted in Texas, so the sheriff couldn't pin anything on him. He just chased Lago out of town. He headed straight for the border. He's the fifth gunman to go through El Paso since *El Flagellados* started their troubles.'

'Any new kidnapping lately?'

'No, it's reasonable that the gang takes it easy right now. They've got all that ransom money to wait for.'

'I was just about to mention it. Know anything about the sums to be paid?'

'Not a damn. We'll just have to presume that the parents

have known for some time just how much—and they will get their girls back. They don't dare blab about it, and the police chief in Chihuahua, called Juan de Cordoba by the way, isn't paying much attention to them. He's got kids himself.'

Kane filled his glass again.

'No point in sitting here and waiting for the next move,' he said. 'I've got to get into Mexico some way or another without being seen.'

Zachary emptied his glass and looked at the bottle. Kane shoved it over to him.

'I've been working while you've been sleeping on the train, Morgan,' he said. 'I just got me a great idea.'

'That I'm to be the sixth gunman across the Rio Grande,' Kane added.

Zachary didn't show his disappointment. 'Exactly—but there's more. I made plans with Cordoba and he agrees. The point is, to place you with a man who is very rich and has a daughter he's very fond of. Cordoba knows most of the grandes in Chihuahua. He checked on one he knew of, one who's got a hacienda that's a bit out of the way, tons of pesos and the most desirable daughter in the district. It cost Cordoba days of creeping, crawling, praying and threatening before her father agreed to it. He's called Don Salvatore Marco and he's as proud as a Castilian cock. He didn't like the idea of his beloved daughter acting as some kind of bait. Finally, Cordoba convinced him that that wasn't the case and that we were only going to protect her. And he explained that he'd have to place a man at Marco's place.'

'Okay,' Kane said. 'But Chihuahua is big. I can sit on my arse for weeks while "the whipped ones" are stealing girls all around. It seems a pretty weak plan, Ed.'

'It is,' Zachary agreed. 'But what in hell are we gonna do? Whip you and get you into the gang that we know nothing about? Believe me, Kane—we've tried everything.'

Kane took a sip of whisky and water. He said,

'Up to now "the whipped ones" have only operated in Chihuahua—right?'

'Yes. That's why we think the gang's from Texas.'

'Well, that sounds reasonable. How many large haciendas are there in Chihuahua?'

Zachary fished a paper from his inside pocket. 'About a dozen. If you're wondering why we don't put a man on every hacienda I'd just like to explain that I've already thought of it and Shane laughed and asked if I was drunk by thinking that he had fifteen men he could send off on a small, crappy case like this! Small! Get that!'

Kane guessed that Shane didn't give two hoots if rich Mexicans lost their daughters. That he was concerned with the case so early was because he was afraid that it might develop into a quarrel between Mexico and Texas. He mentioned it to Zachary.

'Oh, sure! Shane's a sly bastard. If two men can do the job he's happy.'

Kane nodded. He was slightly intoxicated.

'Back to these kidnappings,' he said, 'can you show me the places on this map?'

Zachary did so. They measured the distances and considered it. 'Three places,' Zachary muttered. 'If we draw a line between these places it looks as if they are the same distance from each other and the same distance from the border.'

'Where is Marco's hacienda?'

Zachary pointed to a place about fifty kilometres north of the town called Aquiles Serdan and thirty kilometres west of the Rio Bravo ... or Rio Grande as it's called in Texas.

Zachary looked up. 'Doesn't look as if we chose the worst place, eh, Kane?'

'Looks okay to me.'

It was okay too. Marco's hacienda lay, in fact, like the fourth spot on a line that passed through the other places, almost parallel with the border going north to south.

'Looks as if they're keeping within a distance of about sixty to a hundred and twenty miles from the Rio Grande and border,' Kane said. 'Think they're heading over the border with the girls?'

'No idea.'

'No, that doesn't sound right somehow,' Kane mused. 'It'll be too far to go with the ransom money.' He looked at the map again. The country around Rio Conchos and further north towards San Andres and Buenaventura lay to the east of the mighty Sierra Madre mountains. An 'Eldorado' for hunted men.

Zachary followed his gaze.

'Sierra Madre,' he nodded, 'I quite agree.'

Kane looked up. 'This Marco must have a small army of vaqueros?'

'About two hundred.'

'Hm,' grunted Kane.

Zachary glanced at Kane. 'What's on your mind?'

'Nothing special.'

Zachary emptied his glass. 'If you're heading over the border as a gunman then we'll have to arrange it in such a way that it'll be watertight,' he said. 'Tomorrow you must make sure you get pushed out of town by the sheriff with as much commotion as possible. El Paso is a big town, and as it ain't normal to go naked to the waist just about anyone could be one of "the whipped ones".'

Kane smiled. 'Okay.'

'Eaten dinner?'

'No.'

'Then let's go to the Del Oro—it has the best Mexican food in the world.'

'Okay.'

Kane changed his clothes and stuck his holster down in the lining of his trousers. He buttoned up the light-weight, dark jacket and grabbed his flat-crowned Stetson.

They went out.

It was already dark. But the heat was almost as intense and the slight breeze would hardly make it cooler before dawn again. The streets were full of people and they could hear laughter and curses and music pouring out from the saloons and gambling joints.

The Del Oro was a Mexican café that was run by two

sisters that together weighed almost two hundred pounds, or so Zachary guessed. The place had an earthern floor, stone walls and thick, sooty roof beams. The floor and walls were covered by Mexican blankets and a few Navaho blankets of fine quality. Thick, moulded candles were stuck in the necks of brown tequila bottles. The tables had stone slabs and empty whisky barrels served as stools. The table cloths were of brick-red hessian.

They sat in a corner.

They ordered lamb cut in strips and fried in onions and pepper, boiled chicken in pepper sauce, and to go with the meal a dusty bottle from the café's treasure chest in the cellar.

They ate in quietness and exchanged just a few remarks on the wine and food. Zachary took a green pepper and chewed on it thoughtfully in silence. Kane followed suit. Years of training had taught him to accustom himself to this indigestible food.

They ordered tequila. Saucers of salt appeared on the table. They poured a little salt on the palms of their hands, licked at it and quickly emptied the glass. The liquor burned their throats and left a warm, comforting feeling in their bodies.

Zachary chatted about El Paso, the surrounding countryside and people he knew. Kane wondered if he was talking to make him relax. He couldn't bear the thought of riding into proud Chihuahua and play baby-sitter for a Spanish grande. The thought of hanging around a hacienda like some kind of scum just wasn't to his liking. Kane knew from experience that really proud Mexicans of the old, titled Spanish families were impossible to live with. Let alone their women. Just a passing glance was taken as an attempted rape. He remembered an episode that had happened ten years previously when he was just about to seduce a beautiful girl and a group of vaqueros had caught them. Kane had only just avoided death. What happened to the girl he never found out but he guessed that she would have been spared as she still had her virginity in one piece.

He realised that Zachary was staring at him across the table.

'I forgot to mention one more thing,' Zachary said quietly. 'Only Marco himself knows that you're a U.S. marshal. To the others you're just a hired gun—a revolvèro. It'll be to your detriment all the time but at least we're sure that nobody blabs.'

'That's fair enough.'

Zachary chuckled. 'Feel like a hand of cards—before you, let's say, enter the jaws of death?'

Kane nodded.

They called for Rosa, gave her a large tip and left, with her cries of many happy years and healthy strong sons, ringing in their ears.

'They're strange that way,' Zachary said with a laugh, 'they measure happiness in appetite and sexual ability.'

They chose a place that bore the humble name of The Golden Gift—a huge, roomy place decorated in white, light blue and white, a poor copy of the elegant French-inspired gambling saloons in the Creole quarter of New Orleans.

Black-Jack was played there and poker and roulette. 'Hostesses' in the minimum of clothing with low-cut dresses and deep splits showed the guests to their tables.

A tall, red-haired woman with the greenest eyes Kane had ever seen smiled and came across towards them, with a soft, swaying motion of her hips.

'Good evening, gentlemen,' she smiled professionally. 'Which game do you prefer?'

'Anything—as long as you are part of the winnings,' Zachary smiled.

She curtsied elegantly. 'Sorry, sir—I'm part of the inventory here.'

'Then please pay my compliments to the architect, Miss!'

Kane couldn't help smiling. Zachary was in great form.

She looked into Kane's grey eyes. 'Your friend has some

difficulty in choosing,' she said. 'Perhaps you are more decisive?'

Zachary almost shuddered. There was both invitation and challenge in her eyes and both of them were glued to Kane.

Kane smiled slightly.

'I prefer poker.'

The green eyes smiled at him. 'I thought so. You're the poker type, sir.'

'Am I?'

Zachary shook his head. He couldn't understand this at all. He glanced at Kane. Could his cold eyes and brutal expression appeal to women? He reluctantly had to admit to himself that it may be so. As they walked across the floor Zachary began to look at his friend from a woman's point of view—the slim, almost skinny body, the small head with the high cheek bones, the slate-grey eyes and the passionate lines around the mouth—Yeah, Zachary thought with resignation—it's not just on the firing range that Kane stands out!

With a wave of her hand she bade them sit at a round table covered in the traditional green felt.

'In a moment three more gentlemen will be arriving,' she said. 'If you wish for anything to drink, you can just order it here. By the way,' she said with a glance at Kane, 'I'm called Trace. Trace Miller.'

'Kane.'

'Zachary.'

She smiled and walked slowly back to the bar.

Kane rolled a thin, light-brown cigarette and lit it. His eyes flashed quickly around the room. It looked as if he had forgotten Trace already.

Zachary pulled his chair up nearer. He wondered if he ought to inform Kane that he had the woman in the palm of his hand and was only a hair's breadth from her bed already, but something told him to drop it.

Trace Miller led three men over to the table. They were introduced and then the game started. Trace moved over to a palm that was standing on a table. She leaned carelessly across the table. Kane's dark head was bowed over his cards. She hoped he would win. She hoped he would stay a while in The Golden Gift—and in El Paso.

Exactly half an hour after they had been playing Kane put his cards slowly down on the table and stared at the young, heavily-built man in the dark suit who sat opposite him. Zachary raised his head quickly—feeling instinctively that something was about to happen.

Kane said quietly, 'I'm just advising you to keep your hands real easy. Just lay down your cards, get up and get the hell outa here!'

The other players glared at Kane. Zachary kept his eyes on the other man opposite Kane. He saw the calculating look he gave Kane, saw the way he was wondering whether to take the threat seriously or not.

'How's that, mister,' he said, 'don't like the taste of losing or somethin'?'

'You're cheating,' Kane said.

The man stared at Kane, never taking his eyes off him. He still had both hands on the table. But the deep lines around his mouth showed how tense he was.

'That's a dangerous accusation, mister,' the man who had introduced himself as Lawton, said. 'You ready to take the consequences for it?'

'Keep your hands of your gun, Lawton,' Kane said, 'the marks in those cards are so deep they're collecting dust. Just get the hell outa here so as the air can get freshened up some!'

Lawton rose so quickly his chair hit the ground with a crash. A voice shouted from the bar, 'Gentlemen, please!'

Kane leaned back. As if by some conjuring trick his revolver was in his hand. The barrel was just above the level of the table.

'Drop it,' he said, quietly.

Lawton dropped whatever he was holding under his jacket. A double-barrelled Derringer thudded on the floor. 'You'll pay for this,' he hissed. Zachary kicked the Derringer out of the way. Kane got up, walked around the table and stopped in front of Lawton. He heard an authoritative voice say,

'Hold it right there!'

'It's the sheriff,' Zachary whispered. 'Now's your chance to push it.'

Kane dropped his revolver into his holster, made a half-turn and saw, out of the corner of his eye, Lawton's hairy fist rushing at his heart. He took the punch on his shoulder, stepped inside Lawton's swing and jabbed his left fist into Lawton's solar plexus. The edge of his right hand followed up and chopped the outstretched neck savagely with a loud thud. With a moan Lawton sank unconscious to the floor.

Kane was taken by the collar and swung around.

'Hold on, sheriff!' Zachary shouted loudly.

A crowd of inquisitive onlookers had gathered around them. Trace Miller looked from Kane to the unconscious gambler.

Kane met the sheriff's brown eyes. The sheriff's gun was pointed at Kane's belt.

'Gun, mister,' the sheriff said coldly.

Kane took it out and handed it to the sheriff, butt first.

'Trouble-maker, eh?' he sneered. 'El Paso's better off without types like you. What's your name, mister?'

'Kane.'

'Oh yeah ... Kane, eh?' The sheriff exchanged glances with Ed Zachary. 'All right, Kane ... I know a skunk by his smell. By twelve tomorrow you'd better have your hide outa El Paso—or I'm coming for you! Get it?'

Kane nodded. 'Got it.'

The sheriff weighed the Colt in his hand. 'You'll get this back at my office when you leave. All right, folks—the show's over.'

The sheriff marched towards the door. Three of the saloon workers dragged Lawton out of the room. A deputy followed them. The crowd dispersed and the game went on.

Zachary muttered out of the corner of his mouth:

'Couldn't have been planned better, eh?'

'Was it planned?'

'No, are you crazy?' Zachary smiled.

They broke it up around two o'clock in the morning. The place was almost empty. Zachary counted the money in front of him.

'Forty dollars,' he said. 'I'm gonna end up rich this way . . . forty!'

Kane piled up his winnings . . . about five hundred. A couple of men went around turning off the oil lamps. It was quite dark.

'Closing time, gentlemen! Closing time!'

They got up, thanked the other players for a pleasant evening and headed for the door.

'Real civilised, eh?' Zachary chuckled. 'Something to remember when you're eating dust on the other side of the Rio Bravo, Kane.' Suddenly he narrowed his eyes. 'Just remembered, I gotta talk to the owner of this place. See you tomorrow—okay?'

'All right,' Kane watched him go. He couldn't understand why Zachary suddenly moved off so quickly. Kane shrugged and walked towards the door. When he saw the silhouette there he knew why Zachary had gone.

Trace Miller stood there. He could see the shine of her red hair. Kane frowned. Damn Zachary and his discretion. He didn't need to serve her on a plate.

She came out into the hallway. He stopped and looked at her.

'Your hat, mister,' she said. 'The wardrobe's closed for the night.'

'Thanks.' Kane smiled cynically.

'Were you lucky?' She followed him quite naturally out into the street.

'Yes, thanks.'

It was quiet and dark in the town. A little farther up the street a single ray of light streamed out on to the street. A dog barked somewhere between the houses. The sound made a strange echo.

'I was afraid there was going to be shooting,' she said;

they had stopped automatically on the pavement.

Kane said,

'You can't walk home alone so late. May I escort you, Miss Miller?'

'Thanks.'

They walked a while in silence. 'You're riding on tomorrow?' she asked quietly.

'Yeah—Mexico. I need a vacation,' he said with a hint of a smile.

'Mexico's popular right now. You aren't the first.'

'You don't say.'

She stopped. He could feel her excitement instinctively. He couldn't see her face in the dark.

'Drop in on the way back,' she said. 'Promise?'

'I promise.'

He was about to walk on.

'I live here.'

'Oh . . . well, good night, Miss.'

'Good night.'

He started to go.

'Oh God!' he heard her sigh behind him. 'Do you have to have it in writing?'

He smiled and walked back to her.

CHAPTER FOUR

He followed the Rio Carmen southwards. It was early summer and the land was green and fresh. The lush hills were covered in flowering mesquite and cactus flowers and the air was fresh and clean. The Rio Carmen flowed slowly in lazy meanders through the fertile countryside. The plains alongside the river were flat and the sheep grazing on each side resembled flakes of snow against the green. Light, cream-white clouds drifted across the sky and the wind caressed his ears with a melodic whisper.

It was a beautiful day and Mexico showed its most hospitable and lovely side. Kane enjoyed the ride. He had always liked Mexico—the ridges, mountains, rivers, the small villages, the paved plazas, the church towers, the flocks of sheep and the smiling shepherds' hospitality.

Sitting on the black stallion the way he did he couldn't be anything else except a revolvèro. He was dressed in black from top to toe. His shirt was black, so was his soft, leather vest. He wore black serge trousers, and the half-high, decorated boots were also black.

Round his hips he wore a broad, black gunbelt and his Wayne-Martin holster had been attached to it and tied with a cord to his thigh.

His poise, his clothing, even his horse created a picture of an independent, proud and dangerous man—a revolvèro on the way to a bag of gold pesos ... or a quick death.

Kane had no difficulty in adopting the role of a gunman. The slate-grey eyes had the same watchful, distant look ... and the way he patted the carved butt of the Colt implied that it was a part of himself ... a very important part, perhaps the most important.

That evening he stopped in a village. He noticed that his appearance frightened them. The women pushed the children indoors and the men stayed away. He was given food and a simple bed in the cantina and was on his way again the following day. It was the same everywhere—the black clothing, the challenging gunbelt and his own expression—like a brick wall. Kane smiled to himself—it meant that his appearance was as it should be. It also meant that the average Mexican knew about the lone gunmen that every now and again crossed the Rio Bravo hunting for cash, peace or a safer future.

The fourth day he was stopped by a group of heavily armed vaqueros. In Spanish they explained politely but decisively that he was on Senor Marco's property and would he please mind getting the hell out of it!

Kane explained who he was.

A heavily-built man with crossed ammunition belts over his chest and two revolvers in his belt rode closely up to him. Without taking his eyes off Kane he fished a silver peso up from out of his pocket and put it on his thumb.

'Shoot!' he bellowed, flicking it into the air.

Kane didn't move.

The vaqueros mumbled threateningly and moved nearer. The chief smiled toughly.

Senor, Don Marco pays his revolvèros well. I don't think you are the man for this place. I don't think you are Senor Kane. I think...'

Kane interrupted him. 'Shooting at coins is just circus play,' he said briefly in Spanish. 'It's a game for children. *This* is what it really is...'

He drew like lightning. The revolver thundered three times and three red flowers on a green cactus twenty yards away disappeared in small pieces.

The vaqueros gaped. Kane filled the chambers and dropped the gun back into his holster.

'Take me to Don Marco,' hc said.

'*Si*, senor.'

With an honour-escort of twenty vaqueros Kane rode away—revolvèro Kane—into Don Marco's hacienda.

The house was surrounded by a park of beech, cypress and a few yew trees. Around the hacienda itself was a ten foot high wall of stone. A huge, iron studded door was the only entrance.

A row of heads appeared over the wall. The door opened and the whole group moved in with Kane in the lead.

Kane had seen these rich haciendas before, but he was very impressed by Don Marco's place. It was like a huge, flowering garden. The low, long, white-washed stone house was covered in the loveliest of flowers. In a circle around the house and garden and up against the solid walls stood the rest of the buildings—stables, the servants' quarters, ware-houses and barns.

They rode through an opening in yet another wall and came into the inner plaza. Kane saw that the house was formed like a horse-shoe. Roses climbed up the walls.

Two Mexicans in white came through the doorway in the middle of the patio. Obviously servants. They exchanged a few words with the leader of the vaqueros.

'This way, senor,' one of them said to Kane. 'The men will look after your horse.'

Kane dismounted and walked across the paved patio. It was beautifully cool between the white walls and the smell of flowers was almost over-powering.

He followed them up on to the patio and into a cool, semi-dark hall. Stuffed animal heads were hanging on the walls—huge, black, massive oxheads. Kane wondered if anybody in the Marco family was—or had been—a bullfighter.

'This way, senor.'

He followed the servant through the hall and down a long corridor. The Mexican stopped at the end of it and knocked, opened the door and said with humility,

'Senor Kane, Don Marco.'

'Show him in!'

Kane walked in and the servant shut the door behind him. It was obviously Don Marco's study. The room was dominated by a huge, carved writing desk. Through the open window Kane could feel the breeze caressing his body. On the wall above the writing desk stood a solid bookcase full of books. In front of that were deep, comfortable armchairs upholstered in leather. An open fireplace in the corner would spread a pleasant warmth on cold winter evenings. On the stone floor were carpets and puma skins. Four massive silver candelabras threw flickering shadows on the wall.

'Welcome to my house, senor,' Don Marco said, bowing stiffly.

'Thank you, sir,' Kane answered. It wasn't difficult for him to talk to the Spaniard with respect. Don Marco was not very impressive in build, being small and thin, but the narrow, hawk-like face with the white beard and the hooked, proud nose and the fire and authority in the dark eyes added inches to his height. Kane noticed immediately the barrier between them—it was as hard as iron.

He never attempted to offer his hand to Don Marco; a breaking of the Spanish rules of etiquette like that would never be forgiven. He just stood there with his hat in his hand. And said nothing. He gave Don Marco time to measure him from top to toe.

'My friend the police chief has assured me of your abilities and trust, senor,' he said in perfect English. 'Let me add that I hope his trust in you is worthy of your actions. It is a very ... er ... delicate assignment you have, senor, a fact that Americans perhaps are not aware of.'

'I don't think you have reason to worry, Don Marco,' Kane answered in fluent Spanish. 'Both my boss and I are aware of the nature of this case.'

The Spaniard's face took on a milder expression. It looked as if he had already changed his opinion of Kane while standing there.

'I ask for your forgiveness, senor,' Don Marco said calmly. 'You speak such excellent Spanish I think I am right in saying that you have spent a great deal of time in Mexico, and have quite definitely assimilated some of the spirit and culture that we try to preserve.'

Kane bowed stiffly.

'Sit down, Senor Kane.'

'Thank you.'

When they had taken their seats in the deep armchairs Don Marco offered Kane a cigar. Kane guarded himself against thinking that the Spaniard's conduct was a sign of servility.

'I presume that your assignment is well prepared, senor,' Don Marco went on when the cigars were burning steadily. 'If there should be any question that bothers you, by all means ask me.'

'It's about your vaqueros, Don Marco. How many have you?'

'About two hundred. My *jefè* can give you the exact figure.'

'Well, I presume your men ride great distances now and again—and sometimes far from the hacienda. Is it possible that some of these vaqueros could have heard something or seen something of importance that they haven't noticed in passing?'

'That may be possible. How do you intend to tackle it?'

'Your *jefè*—if I can meet him and talk to him.'

'That can be arranged.'

'Another thing; I would like to know if there's a town nearby, a—let's call it—a dubious place, where some of the bad sort meet.'

'There is, Senor Kane. May I ask what you wish to do there? You will surely find enough distractions here on the hacienda.'

Kane ignored the irony in the Spaniard's tone. 'People often talk indiscreetly in such places,' he answered calmly. 'Sometimes, too loudly too, Don Marco.'

'Excellent,' the Spaniard said. 'The village is called Encinillas. A man called Gonzales runs the cantina there. The place is known for its gambling, whores and killings.'

'Great! I shall just bother you with one more question, Don Marco. Your daughter's habits.'

'Well ... Marguerita is very free. She has few duties and lots of spare time.' Kane saw that he had difficulties saying this and sympathised with him. He knew that the modern Spanish girl lived in constant rebellion against strict parentage. 'She gets up late,' the Spaniard went on, 'and takes a ride after breakfast. Afterwards she has some hours with her governess, then she rests a few hours before dinner. After that she has music lessons and often takes a ride in the evening, before supper. The evenings are usually spent in her own room.' Kane noticed a bitter tone behind the words. He realised that Don Marco saw very little of his daughter.

'Who follows her outside the hacienda?'

'Nobody—not at the moment. When she was eighteen years old she refused to ride with the vaqueros.' He was quiet a while and Kane waited patiently. Don Marco gave him a sharp look before continuing.

'Youthful protest and stubbornness usually give strange reactions, Senor Kane. My daughter looks upon herself as a slave. She has said quite clearly that if she is not allowed to ride alone she will NEVER leave her room. She can be most difficult at times, senor.'

'And now?'

'I have accepted her challenge,' Don Marco said. 'I told her that I had hired a—shall we say bodyguard—for her. She laughed in my face. But I don't pay too much heed to it, senor. She is young and fresh and the prospect of spending days in her room can hardly be appealing. She will submit to this and accept you guarding her.'

'She doesn't know I'm a marshal?'

'No, only *I* know your identity, Senor Kane.'

'Good. You mentioned your daughter's governess. How long's she been on the hacienda?'

'Oh ... about five years. She is white, senor. She is originally from the east states, Philadelphia as far as I remember. My daughter is very fond of Miss Taylor.'

'Well,' Kane got up, 'may I thank you for your assistance, Don Marco?'

'I have prepared a guest room in the west wing,' Don Marco said. 'I hope you find the place suitable.'

'If you have nothing against it, Don Marco, I would be grateful to live in one of the huts outside the hacienda.'

The Spaniard was clearly shaken.

'I'm sure you'll find the room more than suitable, Senor Kane and . . .'

Kane took a chance and interrupted him. 'Don Marco, I ask for this because I want to come and go as I wish without disturbing others. Senor, believe me ... it is best for everyone.'

'As you wish. Then permit me to ask the servants to prepare an adobe for you?'

Kane bowed.

'Please go out on to the patio, senor, while I order your adobe. I presume you will want to meet my daughter. She should be finished with her lessons now. I shall inform her that you are waiting on the patio.'

'Thank you.'

'You will find refreshments out there.'

Kane thanked him again. The polite, correct Spaniard had started to get on his nerves and the prospect of meeting a spoiled, self-centred girl didn't make him feel any better. He cursed 'the whipped ones', Don Marco and Shane and Don Marco's daughter in silence.

The Spaniard led him to the broad, open doors and out on to the patio. The pillars, roses, the vines and the low roof seemed wonderfully cool. Light basket chairs and a table stood on the paved stones. A chubby servant girl placed a tray on the table, curtsied with a giggle and disappeared.

Don Marco noticed it and cleared his throat.

'One moment, then she'll be here, senor.'

Kane just nodded. He went over to the table, threw his Stetson on a chair and sat down. He filled one of the glasses and smelled the liquid.

Wine. Cool, sweet wine. He emptied the glass and filled it

again. The cigarette was half smoked when he heard light footsteps on the paved stones behind him. He got up with the glass in his hand and stood looking at her.

Something told him that he was going to have difficulties with Don Marco's daughter, Marguerita.

CHAPTER FIVE

She was quite tall for a Mexican. The full breasts that pressed against the thin, white silk blouse, the dark eyes in the oval face and the ring-covered hand that rested challengingly on her hips, gave the impression of a much older and more experienced woman than Kane had expected.

He bowed slightly.

'My name is Morgan Kane, senorita.'

'And my name is Rita ... senor.' The slight pause between words was enough to make the introduction an insult.

Kane smiled. He never took his eyes off her. He saw that she was studying him closely, almost intensely. The eyes, face, the way she stood—everything showed her undisguised disgust.

'Excuse my curiosity,' she said coldly, 'but it's the first time I've ever seen a revolvèro. In fact I've never seen a coyote, even though I know his howl and bark quite well. Does the wine taste well, Senor Kane? It should do—it's eleven years old. If your taste is more towards bad liquor I'm sure you'll find newly distilled tequila in one of the pigstys outside the hacienda.'

He let her talk, just smoked his cigarette casually and studied the roses and the beautiful garden flowers.

When she stopped he looked at her again.

'Finished, senorita? Maybe we ought to come to the point?'

She came nearer. In the half light she looked breathtaking, but her eyes glittered with evil and hatred. They didn't suit the lovely face. They suited a person who didn't belong to a good Spanish family. Kane knew that if her body was virginal, he couldn't say the same about her spirit.

'What point?'

'That fact that from now on I'm your shadow, senorita.'

Her eyes slid over him, from the boots, up to the deadly gunbelt, to his face. Her eyes hovered on his mouth.

'Your insults are very artistic, but irrelevant,' Kane said calmly. 'Your opinion of me doesn't alter the fact that your father has paid me to do a job—and I intend to do it.'

'Father is old,' she said, cuttingly. 'He should know that loyalty and people's worth can't be bought or paid for. But my father is the master and I must obey his whims—even when it concerns a hired killer like you senor ... a filthy gringo that would have been chased away by the dogs if it wasn't for all this hysteria with El Flagellados!'

'You have quite a turn of phrase, senorita,' Kane answered, ironically. 'Where did you learn it—in the cantina in Encinillas ... or may be in the pigstys outside the hacienda?'

Before he could gather his breath her hand caught the side of his face.

'You'll pay for those words, gringo swine!' she spat, turned on her heel and disappeared quickly into the house.

Kane felt his cheek. His eyes narrowed as he watched her go. Then he smiled. Well, that was that. A suggestion that he leave the hacienda, a short, angry letter to Shane and a good going over when he returned—maybe loss of rank. Damn it, she had managed it—she'd made him angry!

Just as he reached for his hat, he heard footsteps again. He turned, with a look of resignation.

'Mr Kane?' The woman came up to him and offered him her hand. The smile shone from the sweet face. 'You must have made a terrible impression on Rita. She almost ran me down on the stairs! I'm Catherine Taylor. Rita's governess.'

Kane took her hand. It was small, soft and cold.

He smiled down into the blue eyes. 'I'm afraid she managed to do what she intended,' he said lightly, 'to make me mad. Don Marco should be here at any moment to tell me what to do with myself.'

She laughed. Kane noticed the lovely contrast between the teeth and her brown, fresh skin. 'Oh no, Don Marco hasn't paid attention to her tantrums for years. Even his word can't abate Rita's hysteria. But I shouldn't talk like that. You might misunderstand. Rita is really a sweet and lovable girl, Mr Kane. Yes, you may smile, but I've known her for five years. She is stubborn and thinks the hacienda is a prison. If we had changed roles I would have felt the same. She's nineteen—is regarded as a valuable jewel and is guarded as such. She can't help seeing how other girls live; gay, exciting lives ... they have YOUTH, Mr Kane. A youth that, concerning Rita, only the very closest to her are allowed to see.'

Kane twirled the hat between his fingers. There was something about Catherine Taylor, something strained, she talked too quickly, too lightly. Her friendliness didn't seem to suit her background and position in the house. To her Kane was just any old hired killer.

He said:

'You still haven't called me a filthy revolvèro, Miss Taylor. Why?'

'You are far from dirty, Mr Kane and your ability with a gun I know little about. To me you are a man who will guard a girl of whom I am very fond. Would hostility from me pacify you in any way?'

For once Kane felt pushed up in a corner. He smiled and made a slight bow.

'A man like me finds it easy to generalise.'

'Oh? And what kind of man are you?' The smile almost appeared in the brown face.

'We won't talk about me—Rita is more than enough to discuss—for the time being.'

She took the hint without flinching. But there was a suggestion of reservation in the corners of her mouth.

She sat down and arranged her skirt in an elegant bell shape around her. With a wave of her hand she asked him to sit. Kane asked if she would like a glass of wine. They raised their glasses to each other.

'You mentioned Rita's youth,' he said, dryly. 'You can't blame me for wondering why you waste yours teaching a spoiled brat her lessons!'

'Let me quote you, Mr Kane ... it's Rita we should be talking about.'

'Touché ...' Kane smiled. 'All right, she insulted me, I answered her back and she slapped me. Before leaving she swore that I'd pay for it.'

'And you most likely will.' She looked at him and added; 'But I think that you can take it, Mr Kane.'

'Look ... since we're the only whites on the hacienda can't we drop this Mr and Miss business? I'm called Morgan.'

She paused. 'Cathy.'

Kane raised his glass, but she refused to look him in the eyes. Something about her attracted him, her reservation and just-keep-your-distance manner had attracted him. She was sweet without being beautiful, attractive without being overwhelming. There was something ... 'nice' about her, Kane reflected and then disliked the expression he had used. He guessed her to be around thirty. Her face was without flaw and her figure slim and lovely. Just a mature look around her mouth and a hint of melancholy and sadness in the blue, beautiful eyes separated her from a young girl of twenty.

He said:

'Don't be afraid I'll misunderstand, Cathy. I'm aware of what I am and who I am.' That should soften her—if she was interested, Kane thought, doing his best right then. Weeks, maybe months at the hacienda would bore him terribly and an affair with Cathy should be quite interesting. He looked at her mouth and the word 'exciting' came to mind. In a way it was closed, secretive, but there was something about the lines around her mouth that belonged to a woman who had loved—and been loved.

'I never considered that you would misunderstand,

either,' she said calmly. 'I know intelligence when I see it.'

Damn it, Kane thought, typically masculine, after getting his feet caught in his own nets. He'd have to change his opinion of her. She wasn't thinking of making advances to anybody—especially a revolvèro. But okay, he thought, there may be moonlit nights out here on the patio when even an ice-cold governess would melt a little. He was aware of the fact that he was planning the coming weeks as one long vacation. At the moment there seemed little chance that anyone could prevent it either. The hacienda, the walls, the vaqueros—Kane was on the verge of not caring a damn for 'the whipped ones' and all they stood for.

During the evening—when he was settled in the large airy adobe hut and had eaten quite a good meal—he lay on the bed and smoked, taking sips from a jar of tequila. Through the open window he heard sounds from the hacienda.

There was always something special about the nights in Mexico. Kane had often wondered what it was. The darkness, perhaps? The trembling tones from a melancholy guitar? The twinkle of the stars? The laughter of the women? There was a strange, sensual undertone in the sound, challenging, enticing.

He remembered the curious, inviting looks the girls at the hacienda had given him. But he also noticed the threatening eyes of the men, and decided to be careful and keep a cool head.

After Cathy had left him, Don Marco had introduced his jefè to Kane, a huge, bony man in his forties with hanging moustaches and a couple of blinking, black eyes in a pockmarked face. He was called Pedro Arnez. Kane went with him around the hacienda and got to know the buildings and their surrounds. Arnez was an honest, open man and Kane liked him immediately. There was no sign of the jealousy that Kane had feared there might be. It wasn't so stupid to think that a hacienda jefè would feel out of things when an extra security measure was imported from the other side of the Rio Bravo.

They had talked about the country, the people, the villages—and 'the whipped ones'. Arnez informed him that Chihuahua was full of rumours. Rich grandes locked their children indoors and hardly ever rode to church without an armed escort. But nobody had seen anything of them and nobody had heard anything worth looking into. 'Chihuahua is very big, Senor Kane,' Arnez had said. 'Who knows —today maybe they're in Durango, next week Sonora . . .'

Kane wondered if he should air the theory that the gang were maybe on the Texas side of the Rio Bravo but decided to wait. He asked instead about the cantina in Encinillas, if it lived up to its name, and was told that it most certainly did.

'Gonzales is a pig, Senor Kane. His place has been a Mecca for years for Chihuahua's wanted men and criminals. Gringos come there every year and live there a few weeks, yes, even months. Many think they are running from Texas and pay Gonzales for hiding them.'

'Is it far from here?'

'Four hours' ride with a good horse.'

Kane put out his cigarette and rolled a new one. He was dry in the throat. He wanted to go out but remained where he was. The following morning Rita was sure to take a ride. If he wasn't mistaken she'd start being bitchy from the first moment. Kane smiled in the candle-light. Well, if it was a fight she wanted then she'd damn well get one. He felt excited thinking about her. He had no difficulties in remembering their conversation—nor her movements.

He dreamed of her during the night. He woke with a headache and cursed himself for drinking too much tequila the previous evening.

After eating breakfast he wandered across to the stables. He met Arnez there. The foreman smiled broadly.

'Tequila is a hot lover, senor,' Kane said with an answering smile.

Arnez was suddenly serious.

'The senorita rides in half an hour, Kane. Don Marco has

asked me to give you Diablo del Notte.'

The Night Devil, Kane translated mentally. He knew straight away that this horse must be something special and he knew why.

'What's the senorita riding?'

'Her favourite—Diablo Blanco.'

The White Devil, Kane thought, guessing that her horse was a white palomino.

'Fast?'

'Next fastest in Chihuahua.'

Kane smiled crookedly.

'Exactly,' Arnez smiled back, 'only Diablo del Notte is faster . . . I think . . . I hope.' He pointed to the stable where a couple of young boys were having trouble trying to control a horse and lead it out. 'It's Don Marco's own horse, Kane,' he said with a respectful tone. 'A direct descendant from the full bloods that came to Mexico with Cortez. I think that he is more afraid of that horse than anything else.'

'Except his daughter,' Kane said quietly. He looked at the horse with admiration.

It was a huge, coal-black stallion with white socks. It was at least a hand's breadth higher than any other horse Kane had ever seen, and the lines of the body and the way the horse held its head told Kane of terrible power and fantastic speed. The eyes belonged to a devil, proud, angry, vicious with a hint of evil. Kane knew that this steel-hard devil would have to be driven by an iron hand wrapped in silk—just as one drives a woman.

Two men held the horse while the saddle was put on it, a black, silver-studded saddle, the best that Spanish saddle-makers could produce.

Stamping and whinnying from the stable awoke Kane's curiosity. Then they led out a mare, a huge, white, long-legged dream of a mare, in a way lovelier than the stallion, more fascinating, less frightening, a horse a man could love like a person.

'Diablo Blanco,' Arnez said, almost piously.

The stallion flashed its eyes and shook its head violently. A whinny screamed and echoed between the stable buildings. The mare answered with a challenging scream.

'They have children together,' Arnez sighed, 'but they fight all the time, even when they conceived their son. I often think they hate each other—are jealous of each other. Horses are strange creatures.'

Four men had to control the animals. Their hooves hammered the ground, sending dust flying in all directions, their screams disturbing the morning stillness.

'Look at them,' Arnez said. 'Is it hatred between them? Or is it love? Fighting, senor—an eternal fight.'

Kane watched Rita when she came sauntering out with her silver-studded riding whip lashing her sparkling boots impatiently. When she caught sight of the stallion she stopped dead and smashed her boot with her whip, scaring the horses.

'What's the meaning of this, Arnez?' Her voice was like the crack of a whip. 'Who has given you permission to take out Diablo del Notte?'

'Your father, senorita,' Arnez answered calmly. 'Senor Kane is going to ride him.'

There was open hatred in her eyes as she looked at Kane. He said nothing, just stared back. He felt Arnez' uneasy glance on his back.

'Why?' she snapped.

'Maybe he's afraid you'll ride away from your shadow, senorita,' Kane answered. 'I shall promise that I won't be riding away from YOU.'

'Ride from Diablo Blanco?' She laughed. 'NOBODY rides away from her—and certainly not that black murderer there!'

The stallion showed its teeth to her, as if it understood what she said. Kane noticed it. He knew that animals often could feel a person's hatred and wickedness. Was this a warning? He watched her through narrowed eyes as she walked over to the mare. She was dressed in black, tight leather trousers, white silk blouse and black leather jacket decorated with silver thread. She wore a black, flat hat on her head with a silver-studded band under her chin. The black gloves completed the suit. To see a girl of her position in trousers was surprising—and Kane noticed that Arnez looked away. It was clear that he was ashamed of the way she dressed. Kane realised that it must have been a bitter fight for Don Marco to try to make her wear traditional riding clothes before giving up the idea.

Even though he felt antipathy for Rita he couldn't help noticing her body; the long, slim legs, the lush hips and thighs, the round, enticing backside.

She swung up into the saddle, threw a glance at Kane and shouted:

'Now, senor revolvèro! Goodbye ... and thanks for the visit!'

She dug in her spurs in the mare's side. The horse screamed with pain, and the stable boys jumped aside as the mare tore away like white lightning across the yard and disappeared between the trees.

Without losing a second Kane was in action. He leapt into the saddle, shouted at the top of his voice and dug the long spurs deep into the horse's flanks. He felt the mighty muscles tremble, then the animal sprang into action. The acceleration was so powerful that Kane swayed backwards. The pull on the reins was so hard he knew that the animal had a jaw of steel. He got his feet into the wide leather stirrups and got a better grip of the reins. He was glad he was wearing gloves or the stallion would have torn the skin off his hands. Then he was between the trees and heading for the wide-open gate and he saw Diablo Blanco like a white fleck out on the green plain.

He lay forward along the horse's neck like a jockey. The stallion began to stretch out into a steady gallop and slowly but surely he crept up on Rita. The plain was even and had a slight growth of low mesquite bushes. Kane saw that she was heading for a slight slope a few miles away. He could see her clearly now, she lay low in the saddle and was using her whip. A white face appeared like a flash and he knew she was looking back.

Now! Kane thought and spurred the black stallion. With a snort the horse increased speed. Its muzzle was stretched out and it kept its head slightly to the right. The enormous muscles worked rhythmically and surely. He was hardly fifty yards from the white mare now. Rita looked back again, then her right arm began to swing up and down. Kane ground his teeth, he hated unnecessary use of the whip on horses. He noticed that the distance between them was the same. The white mare ran like an arrow. Was it aware that Diablo del Notte was close on its heels? Was it running in fear? He spurred the horse again and edged closer. They rode up a slight slope. Both horses were soaked with sweat and foam dropped off the mare. As the horses passed the hill-top, Kane was alongside the white mare. He let the stallion edge forward a couple of lengths and then began to slacken off slightly. He reckoned on her doing the same and swore when he heard the sound of her whip against wet horse's flanks. Rita swore in Spanish, so loudly that he could hear it above the hammering hooves. She shot past him like an arrow and on towards the green flatness of the valley where a river meandered lazily along.

Kane spurred the horse again, furious now. He was soon alongside the exhausted mare, forced the stallion up against it, leaned out of the saddle and gripped the mare's bit. Rita's wet, sweat-soaked face was turned towards him, her hand swung out and her whip caught him across the face.

'Let go, you swine!' she screamed.

Kane pulled in the mare with all his might. The stallion seemed to understand what he was trying to do because it planted all four legs stiffly into the ground and literally slid forward in a shower of turf and grass.

Once again the biting pain of the whip tore across his cheek, then the speed had decreased to such an extent that he could ease the pressure on his right arm. When she attempted to whip him for the third time his hand shot out and tore the whip out of her hand.

The black and the white horses stood still, their foaming

sides rising and falling violently. Their nostrils were blood-red.

Kane still held the mare's bit.

'How dare you!' she screamed almost hysterically. 'I'll have you whipped for this, you swine ... you disgusting gringo swine!'

'Clam up!' Kane sneered, swinging down from the saddle without releasing the bit. Without paying any attention to her cursing he began to loosen the saddle and girth strap on the mare. The saddle began to slide off and she had to jump down so as not to fall. Kane looked at the mare—it was almost all in. It bore marks of the whip along its flanks and bleeding gashes made Kane look at her spurs. Her boots were speckled with blood.

He stared at her, his eyes narrowed in anger.

'Why the hell don't you shoot the horse if you damned well want to kill it,' he said coldly. 'Or is a bullet too humane?'

'That's not your business! What right have ...!'

Kane interrupted her brutally. 'I told you to clam up! And don't think I'm gonna listen to your crap right now, Rita!'

She laughed, shortly, angrily, her neat boots stamping the grounds. 'Pig! Swine! Just wait until my father hears about this ... he'll have you whipped, he'll tear the hide off you, drive you out of Mexico like a dog! If it hadn't been for you ...' She turned and kicked the horse savagely on one of its hind legs. 'If it hadn't been for you I ...'

She didn't get any further. A hand gripped her shoulder and swung her round and before she knew where she was she was lying across his knee on her stomach.

Kane gave her a stinging switch across her backside with the whip. It cracked loudly but her scream was louder. She twisted and turned, kicked and fought but Kane held like a vice and used the whip until her screams turned to cries and her cries to hysterical sobbing. Then he threw her to one side and stood looking at her with the whip in his hand. Her shoulders rode and fell quickly but he was still burning with anger.

She lay on her face sobbing with pain, her fingers buried in the grass.

'Now you know how the horse felt,' Kane sneered. 'And let me add no matter what the consequences are of this I wouldn't have missed it for the world!'

The horses rolled in the grass. A couple of waders rose from the river bank and flew low over the valley. He lit a cigar and sat on a grassy mound. Now and again he glanced over at the slim figure. She was lying almost quietly now, her body twitching now and again as she sobbed heavily. Kane got up and went across to the mare. She looked much better now. He stroked the smooth neck and talked softly to it. The mare snorted and rubbed her muzzle against his hand. Once again the anger boiled up in Kane and if Rita as much as raised her head right then, he would have gone mad again with the whip.

The black stallion was grazing some way away. It was almost dry now. Kane had to swallow—what a horse! His thoughts went to Don Marco. The Spaniard must trust him a lot. What a temptation a horse like that was for a man!

But the mare would have to be treated, the sores disinfected and the stiffness worked out of it.

'Get on your feet,' Kane said.

She didn't move.

He went over to her, grabbed her by the arms and dragged her to her feet like a rag doll. Her face was white and grimy with tear stains. Then new life appeared in her eyes.

'Don't you dare touch me!' she snapped.

Kane shook her until her head lolled on her shoulders, her hair dishevelled.

'Stop it!' she whimpered. 'For God's sake . . .'

He stopped.

'Stand right here,' Kane said. 'Got that?'

She spat right in his face.

Kane hit her quickly, open handed. She was knocked flying, came up on her feet again and cursed him venomously. The left side of her face began to swell.

With narrowed eyes Kane went over to her, grabbed her hand that was clawing at his eyes and smacked her across the face again.

This time she stayed down.

Kane got hold of the stallion, threw the other saddle over the saddle horn and tightened the girth strap. He led the stallion over to her. The mare followed him.

'Get up,' Kane said coldly.

She barely raised her head. She was breathing heavily.

'I said get up!'

She got to her feet.

Kane said,

'You can lie trussed up across the neck or sit behind. What's it to be?'

Her eyes were clear again now. She stared intensely at him, the dark, hard face, the glittering, grey eyes, the brutal lines of the mouth. An expression of fear, almost submission came into her eyes.

She nodded.

Kane swung into the saddle and gave her his hand. 'Jump up,' he said.

He had to pull her up to him.

The stallion trotted away, the mare following. It looked as if the wildness had been burned out of the animals. Kane smoked his cigar and squinted out across the green plains. Far out to the west he could see the violet silhouette of the Sierra Madre. An almost invisible flash told him of the snow-capped peaks.

Rita sat behind him. She swayed slightly and tried to hold on to the saddle. But the leather was smooth and her fingers without power. Twice she almost fell off. The third time Kane turned in the saddle, put a long arm around her and pulled her forward in front of him. For a moment her body was stiff with resistance, then she relaxed and almost sank against him.

The sun moved across the sky and the mild wind whispered in their ears. The birds sang in the bushes, and in the distance a flock of sheep were bleating.

Kane glanced down at her. Her dark head lay against his shoulder. He caught a glimpse of her face. It was pale, dirty, tear-stained. Her eyes were closed.

Poor little devil, he thought...

'An accident with the girth strap,' he told the vaqueros that came to take the horses in the hacienda. 'The senorita fell off but is not hurt.'

She stood there looking at him as they led away the horses. Her eyes were on the marks on his face from her whip.

Kane said quietly, 'Thanks for the ride, senorita. I'm sure that your father will be interested in your ... fall.'

Something resembling a sob came from her throat, then she whirled round and disappeared towards the house.

CHAPTER SIX

Rita didn't show herself during the following three days. She had her meals served in her rooms. Kane passed his time riding around the property, chatting to the vaqueros and emptying a bottle of tequila or two with Arnez. He seldom saw Don Marco, but he saw Cathy Taylor often...

'I wish I knew what happened on that trip,' she said the fourth day. Rita still hadn't appeared.

'Must something have happened?'

'She's never been like this before.'

'Maybe she's never fallen so hard before,' Kane answered.

The same evening he decided to ride to Gonzales' cantina in Encinillas. Don Marco had let him borrow Diablo del Notte whenever he wished as long as he was staying at the hacienda and Kane thanked him politely. He still didn't know if Don Marco had heard about the riding trip. Kane had been about to ask many times. But the Spaniard was so polite, distant and correct. If he was angry about Kane's treatment of his daughter then he hid it well.

Kane rode to Encinillas in just over two hours. Those two hours were enough for him to fall completely—he was just full of admiration for the black stallion. And the strange thing was that the feeling was mutual. Kane thought about the colourful tales the vaqueros had told him about the horse's moods, wickedness and almost human slyness. He could hardly believe that this was the same horse, it obeyed the slightest pressure of the spurs and twitch of the reins. Kane was in a good mood when he saw the lights from the town down in the valley.

The town had maybe two hundred inhabitants, four or five dusty streets and half a dozen cantinas.

Kane rode slowly up the 'main street', which was narrow and dusty. Along the walls of the houses were hitching posts and he saw at least four branded horses with American saddles. It was so dark that nobody paid much attention to him and Kane tied the horse up carefully outside the town's largest cantina where a sand-blown sign told him that it was Gonzales' cantina.

Kane had seen dozens of them; earthern floors, oil lamps, dirty tables, dirtier whores and a couple of gangs bent over their cards. They looked up when he arrived, followed him with their eyes across the floor to the lone table in the corner, only to concentrate on the cards again when he sat down with his face to the door and his back against the wall.

A plump whore came over to him. A short exchange of words told her where to go. Kane was given a few theories about his parentage, especially on his mother's side. He waved to a filthy Mexican in shabby clothing and ordered tequila and salt on a saucer.

'Passing through, senor?'

'Yeah.'

'In a hurry?'

'Just get the tequila, man, and fast!'

'Si, senor ... at once.' The man bobbed away, glancing backwards with hate-filled eyes. The card gang dealt their cards again. Kane looked at them. Six whites. All young—at least under forty. They were heavily armed. There was gold on the table in front of them. Kane noticed a pile of golden twenty dollar coins. He rolled a cigarette and thought of the horses he had seen. Most had ranch brands he knew from Texas. The horses should belong to common cow-hands at forty dollars a month.

Then he noticed the eyes of one of the men. He was young, maybe the youngest of them all, blond, lightly built and very handsome. He stared stiffly at Kane. He knocked the cards against the table in a steady, monotonous rhythm.

One of the others said something to him. Kane caught the name 'Babe'.

'Babe Lago,' Zachary had said, 'gunman from Nueces—in the same class as Buck Duane and John Wesley Hardin . . .'

Kane took a sip of the tequila. He felt his nerves reacting to Lago's glance. Did the guy think he was a sheriff who had followed him here to Mexico?

Kane cursed himself for having decided to ride to Encinillas. What if Lago wanted to fight? The rumour of the fight would spread over all Chihuahua and Texas faster than a horse could ride. And the result? Kane felt a sinking in his stomach and had to swallow to get rid of the sudden dryness.

Another of the players turned and looked at Kane. He said something to Lago in a low voice. Lago sneered and placed his cards face down.

'Feel like a hand, stranger?' he asked in a high voice.

Kane paused and thought about it. 'Thanks.'

They made room for him. Kane knew that they were inviting him only to get a closer look at him. None of them introduced themselves so Kane just nodded to them. He noticed that about half the coins looked newly minted.

With traditional beginner's luck Kane took the pot with three nines. He threw away in the next hand but held on to the last in the third. Lago had 'seen' him and had put down three aces. Kane stared into the young man's blue eyes as he threw his four queens down.

Lago leaned back in his chair. He was dressed only in black—like Kane—and his face seemed narrow, pale and childish. But his eyes were self-assured and cold.

'Got a lucky streak, mister.'

'Looks like it,' Kane answered. It was his turn to deal and while he dealt and shuffled he checked, routinely, to see if the cards were marked. They weren't. He gave himself two fours and three crummy cards. He decided to stay in the running and bought three cards. Another four and two jacks. House. Pretty sure to be a winner. Four men stayed and after two rounds the pot was up around six hundred dollars.

'Raise two hundred,' Lago said.

Kane followed up. The others swore and threw in their hands. Bad tactics, Kane reflected, he would have followed up and tried to bluff it—if he, of course, had enough money to complete the bluff.

Lago smiled slightly. 'Looks like it's just you and me, mister.'

Kane nodded. 'Want more?' he asked, knocking the ash off his cigarette. He knew that a casual gesture like that would have an irritating effect when there was a thousand dollars on the table. That was why he did it.

'Raise two hundred,' Lago said, his voice now getting slightly hoarse.

'And two hundred more,' Kane answered. He looked around. 'Excuse me, boys, I'll just fetch my bottle.'

Lago placed his hands flat on the table and leaned forward. 'Drink mine, mister!'

Kane looked at him. 'All right,' he nodded and took the bottle. He filled his glass and emptied it. Then he began to roll a cigarette. Lago was shiny with sweat on his upper lip and forehead.

The others sat quiet, dead quiet. Kane noticed that they glanced at him, then at Lago and back to him again.

Kane lit his cigarette. 'Well.'

Lago covered the hand. 'I'll see you, mister,' he hissed.

Kane put down his cards.

Lago swore bitterly and threw his cards on the floor. He had a full house too—three twos and two eights.

Kane gathered up the cash. Lago stared at him, pale with anger, but with an excited look in his eyes.

'You play well, mister,' he said thinly. 'That your job?'

Kane laughed. 'No, not exactly.'

'You working here?'

'Nope.'

'Passing through?'

'Uhuh.'

'To or from?'

'To or from what?' Kane glanced at Lago. He could read the youth like a book. He had seen that sort of rage before not to know what it was all leading to.

Lago's hands were shaking. 'To or from the border!' he snapped.

'What's that with you?'

'I like to know who I lose money to!'

'And I like to know who I'm taking money *from.*'

'Lago's the name. Babe Lago. Are you a damned sheriff?' The table was showered in spittle as Lago shouted it. The other men tensed, ready to dive aside in a second if things got too hot.

'No,' Kane answered. He smiled and added: 'I could say, far from it, in fact.'

Lago's shoulders that had been hunched slowly sank.

'Explain yourself, mister,' he said, huskily. 'We like straight people here at Gonzales'. Right, Pepe?'

'Right,' said a soft, Mexican voice behind Kane. He turned slowly and saw a huge, pock-marked man in silver-embroidered vest and elegant leather trousers. His right hand hung over a silver-studded revolver in his belt.

'Name, mister,' Lago sneered.

Kane looked at him across the table.

'Kane,' he answered.

'Any more?'

'Morgan.'

Lago paused. Clearly, the name meant nothing to him and Kane hadn't expected it to either.

'Where are you from?'

'Oh . . . out east.'

Lago said slowly: 'You're smart—much too smart, mister. I don't like smart people!'

Kane stared into his eyes. 'So what do you intend to do about it?'

Lago got up slowly with his hands on the table. His slim, small body shook with tension.

'Hold on, Babe!' Pepe Gonzales said. 'Remember what

you promised, amigo! No shooting in Encinillas.'

Lago pulled himself together. 'All right,' he hissed. 'All right! But he ain't getting away with it that easily, eh, Pepe? Think we ought to beat some of the slickness out of him?'

Kane never moved.

He felt the cold pressure of a revolver barrel on the back of his neck. Then his own weapon was torn from its holster.

'It's a long time since I went a round or two,' Gonzales went on behind Kane's back. 'Get up, mister.'

Kane got up. The gun barrel disappeared from the back of his neck. Gonzales tore off his vest. Beneath the white shirt muscles rippled like snakes. The Mexican smiled: 'Okay with you, Lago?'

'Let her go!'

'Off with your belt, senor,' Gonzales chuckled, self-assured.

Kane unbuckled his belt. By the manner in which Gonzales stood Kane knew that he was—or had been—a fist fighter. Gonzales weighed around a hundred pounds more than Kane and his reach was longer. Kane decided to make the fight as short as possible. Different grips and blows taught him by the Japanese Kiu Yamoto flashed through his head. He'd find use for all of them now—and maybe more.

Gonzales raised his fists in a typical boxing attitude. Kane kept his weight evenly balanced on both legs, his hands half-raised in front of him.

Gonzales didn't wait, stepping quickly up to Kane, feinted with a left to the head, then feinted with another to the body, following up with a short swing at Kane's head. He didn't quite manage to avoid it, the fist glancing off the side of his temple and for a moment he saw stars. He could easily now have brought his knee up into Gonzales' crotch and finished off the fight but he knew that the others would most likely lynch him on the spot. So he hung on to Gonzales instead, until his eyes cleared, then he broke loose, swayed quickly from side to side and jabbed four stiff fingers into the Mexican's gut. Gonzales fought for breath, his mouth open, gasping he went for Kane with his arms swinging. Kane lowered his head between his shoulder blades and took the punches on the arms and shoulders, but kept an eye on the Mexican's movements between the punches. Then he saw an opening, blocked the Mexican's fists to one side and ducked in at him. A sharp jab to the solar plexus, another just above the heart, a chopping blow that missed the throat by a fraction and Gonzales was in trouble. Kane let him gather his senses. Then Gonzales did what he had expected and hoped he would do. Crazy with anger Gonzales tore into him with flying fists and his face distorted with rage. Kane stepped aside, drove his elbow viciously into the Mexican's kidneys and followed up with a crushing punch to the heart. The air wheezed from Gonzales like a punctured baloon and for a moment he stood there, his arms hanging at his sides. Kane was tempted to punch him in the Adam's apple but instead he gave him one hard, neat punch to the jaw. Gonzales was paralysed, sank to his knees, swung round and fell on his face with a crash.

It was deathly quiet in the cantina.

Then Babe Lago swore hysterically.

'Hold it, Babe!' The voice was like the crack of a whip. Kane turned. A tall, lean figure at the other card table got up.

'Ain't nothin' to do with you, Clay! Keep outa this!' Lago screamed, his hand hanging like a claw over his revolver.

'Gonzales said no shooting,' said the one called Clay. 'It was a straight fight, Babe. If you feel like it, you can try next time!'

Kane stared at Clay. He noticed that the man was peeling around the nose, forehead and ears.

Gonzales sat up, his eyes trying hard to focus again. Then he caught sight of Kane and tried to smile. It was more a twisted grimace.

'Where in hell did you learn to fight, senor?' he grunted,

climbing to his feet.

'A cook taught me,' Kane answered.

Gonzales said: 'Give him his gunbelt back.' He looked at Kane as he buckled on the belt. 'A drink, Kane? On the house, of course.'

'Thanks.'

They walked over to the bar.

Babe Lago stared at Clay. 'Next time,' he whispered, 'next time...'

'Any time, Baby,' Clay answered and sat down again. The light from the lamp threw a sharp light over the patches of peeled skin on his face. He had pulled the cuffs of his shirt far down over his hands. They also showed sore patches.

Kane glanced at him.

'Who's my guardian angel?'

'Clay. Clay Sanderson. A quiet, nice guy. He's been around a few weeks.'

Kane tried to attract Sanderson's attention but he had already gone back to his game again.

Gonzales said: 'If you're interested in staying, that's okay.'

'I'll be back in again,' Kane answered, watching Sanderson the whole time. There was something about the patches on the face that disturbed him.

He chatted for a few minutes to Gonzales. Then he understood that he made his living by putting up men like these, not asking any questions into the bargain. But Kane couldn't forget the fact that it wasn't like Mexicans to take a defeat that easily.

He grabbed his hat. Babe Lago looked up, his eyes shining with hatred.

'Buenas Noches,' Kane said. 'I'll be back—if that's okay with you, Gonzales.'

'That's okay.' The Mexican's smile didn't reach as far as his eyes. 'We'll be waiting for you, Kane.'

Clay Sanderson looked up when Kane left. He watched him until the door closed behind him. Then he raised his hand and scratched himself on the shoulder.

It was a habit he had picked up.

His scars were itching.

A couple of hours after Kane had left Encinillas, Clay Sanderson got up, gathered his money and grabbed his hat.

Gonzales looked at him.

'A moonlight trip, amigo?'

'Dolores is starting to kick up a fuss,' Sanderson said. 'She says I play too much poker and lie with her too little.'

'Buenas Noches,' Gonzales chuckled.

Babe Lago grabbed the bottle after Sanderson had left. He started to drink quickly—as if in a hurry to get drunk.

Sanderson saddled his horse and rode northwards. He didn't ride fast. He used his eyes and ears well and when he reached the Santa Clara river he was sure that he wasn't being followed. He followed the river bank for a while.

An hour later he was sitting in a large, well-lit room and staring into the eyes he had learned to fear.

'And he's called Kane?' The voice was deep and melodic.

'Morgan Kane.'

'Describe him, Clay.'

'Tall, lean. About a hundred and fifty, hundred and sixty pounds. At a guess around six foot four inches in height. High cheek bones. Grey eyes. Carries just one Colt in the usual belt holster. Dressed in black.'

'Sure he's no sheriff?'

'Well, he sure wasn't after any of us. I wondered about Lago, but he didn't try anything. When Lago wanted to try him I stopped it. I thought you'd want to wait a while.'

'That was wise of you, Clay! Yes, this man interests me.' The black, sparkling eyes stared into Sanderson's blue-grey eyes. 'Find out where he's staying.'

Sanderson nodded. 'He said he'd be back to Encinillas soon.'

'Good. We'll put him to the test then. Worry Lago, Clay. Tease him. We have no use for him at all. If Kane kills him, I'll consider your proposal.

'Oh, one more thing, Clay. Don't let Babe Lago think

that it's YOU who want him to take Kane. Just get him going, that's all. Nobody must comprehend what is behind all this.'

'I see.'

'Must you return?'

'Not straight away.'

'I've got a new girl for you, Clay—just to show how much I appreciate your work.'

'Thanks, boss.' A gleam of desire in his eyes caused the other man to chuckle.

'The time you spent as a celibate was difficult to live through ... wasn't it, Clay?'

'Yeah, boss. But I'm catching up slowly.'

Kane knew that he might be followed. The night was mild, dark and quiet. Now and again he stopped the horse and listened, knowing that all sounds would carry far that night. But he heard nothing, and let the stallion make its own pace. His thoughts wandered to the men in the cantina. There was something unreal about the whole business, the poker gang, the chuckling Gonzales, the young gunman from Nueces—and Clay Sanderson ... the man who was peeling all the time. That was pretty unusual. Sanderson didn't have red hair and shouldn't that pale, sensitive skin belong to a red head? Why had his skin been so sensitive to the sun? A good guess would be that he had spent a good deal of time in the shade. In a prison, for example.

Hm, Kane thought.

He was also wondering why Sanderson had stopped Babe Lago from going for his gun.

Why? Certainly not because he was afraid Kane, or even Lago himself, would get killed. Something was behind all this. What? And Gonzales—why did he want Kane to come back again? To get a chance at beating him at poker? Maybe. But Kane wasn't convinced. Encinillas had the reputation of being a hang-out for the lawless. Gonzales not wanting any shooting in his place didn't quite fit the picture.

Kane decided to pay Encinillas another visit.

The hacienda was dark and quiet when he returned, except for faint lights from a couple of adobe huts. He led the horse into the stable. Two of the stable boys woke up and Kane asked them to give the horse a good brush down. They smiled and nodded.

'Buenas Noches, senor,' they shouted as he walked away.

Kane walked slower as he neared his own door—an old habit. He put his toes down first and literally slid along quietly on the soles of his feet. He walked quietly up to the door and pushed it open. For a moment his throat turned dry and his nostrils quivered. The odour of perfume was overpowering. He stood there in the darkness, trying to pick out features in the dark room. He realised that she must be in the small alcove behind the curtain. Moonlight would have revealed her in the larger room. Kane slipped quietly through the door and shut it behind him, slowly. He moved along the wall until he was standing beside the curtain. He leaned forward and peeped in. The smell of perfume there was even stronger. He heard someone breathing slowly, steadily.

She was asleep.

Kane fetched the lamp, carefully guarded the match and then lit it. Not a sound came from the alcove. He unrolled the mats over the windows and got the lamp to burn clearly. Then he walked over to the curtain and pulled it aside. He raised the lamp above his head and stood there.

He was sure that it was going to be Cathy Taylor lying there. But with a shock he saw that the black, long hair must belong to a Mexican girl. She had pulled the blanket up around her and lay facing the wall. By the way the blanket was shaped he knew that she was slim and young.

He hung the lamp on a hook and stood there wondering what to do. It must be a girl that Arnez had sent. Damn his eyes!

Kane glanced at what he could see of the face. Curious, he moved nearer.

It was Rita.

It was as if someone had thrown a bucket of cold water over him. He stood there, unsure of what to do. So near to being lynched he had never been. If one of the stable boys had seen her go to his hut ...! And what the hell was she doing here anyway? He was boiling with anger. Spoiled little bitch ... so she hadn't given up hope of breaking him! At any moment she'd scream and yell for help, saying he'd dragged her there by force, tried to rape her or something similar. He had to get her out of there—and fast. For a moment he wondered if he should knock her senseless and carry her back to the house—but how would he get her in without being noticed?

Suddenly she woke and turned to him. They stared at each other in silence for a few seconds. Her eyes were dark and heavy with sleep. Kane stared at her with eyes glittering with fury.

'All right,' he said, coldly, 'just go ahead and scream!'

She sat up. The blanket fell off her. She was dressed in a dark, velvet suit. She wore a white ribbon in her hair.

'Scream, senor?'

Kane didn't give a damn about the doubt in her voice. 'Why else did you come here—if not to create hell for me? You're going to say I tried to rape you as revenge for the licking I gave you?'

Rita sat up. Her eyes never left him.

'I came to apologise,' she said, coldly. 'I thought I owed you an apology—but I see now that it is completely wasted on a man like you, with your vulgar ways and animal thoughts ...'

'How did you get in here?' Kane barked. 'Did anyone see you?'

'Afraid, senor revolvèro?' Her smile mocked him.

'I've got other things to think about ...' He stopped and reached for the lamp. 'Come here. You're going back—and fast!'

She got up and stretched slowly and lazily like a cat. Kane grabbed her arm and shoved her out into the other room.

'That hurts, senor ...'

'Shut up!' Kane opened the door slightly and peered out. 'Come here, I'll follow you up to the house.'

'I'm not afraid of the dark, senor ...'

Kane didn't answer, just grabbed her arm and dragged her after him. He walked so fast that she had to almost run beside him. He could hear her laughing quietly to herself, mockingly. 'The brave revolvèro runs like a hare,' she said. 'And I was so impressed by the way you used a whip on a woman, senor ...'

'I told you to clam up!' Kane hissed, angry at her and himself and the ridiculous role he had to play. If it hadn't been for the job—and the star in his back pocket—he would have kissed her until she bled and then have kicked her out of the hut. But he had to think of his own safety first and not give a damn for his pride.

They rushed through the dark garden up to the rear of the house.

'Get inside,' Kane said quietly.

She tore her arm loose and turned to him. 'You're not a man, senor,' she whispered. 'A man would have used the opportunity while he had it. You're a horrible sort of reptile, senor revolvèro—I hope to God that you can use your gun better than you use a woman!'

Kane grabbed her shoulders so hard that he saw her face twitch in pain. Something wild and violent rose inside him, he pulled her so tightly against him that she couldn't breathe and put his face down to hers. With only an inch to spare he whispered,

'If it hadn't been for my job I'd have treated you like the whore you've just been playing! Meanwhile ...'

He kissed her violently. In the slight moonlight he could see her eyes pressed tightly together in pain. She tried to break loose but was as helpless as a child in his grip. And then—when he noticed the resistance disappearing, that her mouth opened hungrily beneath his, that her breath was heavy and gasping, that her arms were locked around him, then he shoved her away and almost had to hold her up. He smiled—a cold, mocking and brutal smile. Without saying a word he turned her round and shoved her towards the patio. She stumbled forward, almost fell and grabbed one of the pillars. Her chest was rising and falling violently. He could see her silhouette. A low sob reached his ears, then the shadow disappeared and he heard a door open and close again.

CHAPTER SEVEN

Arnez looked at him with interest. 'The senorita wishes to ride,' he said slowly.

'Okay,' Kane answered casually. He had a feeling that Arnez was aware of the silent duel between him and Rita. Cathy Taylor too. The evening after Rita had come to his hut, while Kane was strolling around the hacienda, she suddenly appeared in the shadows and stopped some feet away from him.

'Have you two been fighting again?' she asked quietly.

Kane didn't answer.

Cathy came nearer. 'She's crying,' she said quietly. 'All the time. What has happened, Morgan?'

'Why ask me? I've only been out riding with her.'

His voice had a rebuffing tone. Cathy came right up to him. 'She's only a child,' she said. 'You're the first white man she's had any contact with. Try to understand the impression you could make on her.'

He waved his hand impatiently.

'It's true, Morgan. You're a ... an attractive man. You're like a person from another world to Rita, free, independent, strong. She's used to vaqueros who bow at the sight of her. Try to understand, Morgan. For my sake.'

'For your sake,' he repeated.

'Yes. I'm fond of her.'

'Well, if you can make any impression on her, then keep her away from me. I don't like being pushed around—and certainly not by women.'

'Do you despise women?'

He stopped. 'No, but ...'

'She is Mexican,' Cathy said. 'She is a child, bearing a woman's body. Nobody has woken her, Morgan. And YOU mustn't do it.'

His thoughts went back to Rita's passionate kiss on the patio. He moved uneasily. 'Just keep her away from me,' he muttered.

Cathy smiled. 'She's beautiful ... and desirable—isn't she, Morgan?'

Kane looked at Arnez. The Mexican watched him as he thought.

'When?' he asked.

'She'll be here any time.'

And she came, dressed in the same challenging suit as the first time. They rode in silence—he ten to fifteen yards behind her. Once she stopped her horse and sat staring at the distant Sierra Nevada. Kane rolled a cigarette and kept a close watch on her. He was ready for her to try and ride away from him again. But she didn't, she let the white mare trot down into the valley.

When they handed the horses over to the stable boys they still hadn't exchanged a single word. She walked up to the house without looking at him. Kane squinted through his cigarette smoke. This change-over came too suddenly. To hell with her, he thought, cursing the warm feeling in his stomach at the sight of her hips in the tight trousers. She had lit a spark in him—a spark that might break out into flames if he didn't watch himself.

He wandered aimlessly around the hacienda the rest of the day. He met Don Marco in the garden and exchanged a few words with him. Kane had nothing to tell about 'the whipped ones'. The truth was that he hadn't given much thought to the gang in the last few days. The pleasant life on the hacienda and the two women had caught him a little off balance. 'The whipped ones' were something distant and dangerous. He realised that that was how the weeks were going to pass by—nervous inactivity, with Rita's sensual body in his thoughts, enough food and drink and a comfortable hut. It made him irritable. His nature demanded more, dangers, excitement, action. He analysed himself, his character and had to admit reluctantly that he was getting stale. He thought more of Rita's hips and desirable breasts than of practising with his revolver, for example.

It took three hours to ride to Encinillas. Why hadn't he ridden there again and used his eyes and ears? Why had he been satisfied by realising that there was something strange about the place? Why didn't he meet Clay Sanderson again—or Babe Lago? Why wasn't he searching for 'the whipped ones'—instead of following Rita Marco like a trained lap dog?

To hell with the hacienda and to hell with Rita! He'd head for Encinillas that evening—and if anybody threw down the glove he'd sure as hell pick it up and see how far he could go.

The cantina was almost empty. Gonzales smiled broadly when he caught sight of Kane.

'Amigo! Come in, come in. Let me buy you a glass. I've been waiting for you.'

'Why?' Kane answed briefly, taking the glass and tasting the liquor.

'It's boring here,' the Mexican sighed. 'It was different before. There was dancing and music and fights all the time. These hombres who hang around town are afraid of their own shadows. It is a shame—and I lose money!'

Kane saw that Babe Lago was sitting in a corner playing with a deck of cards. Something about his eyes made Kane shudder with expectation. Clay Sanderson was not to be seen.

The door opened and a girl came in, a beautiful and luscious Mexican girl in a colourful skirt and white blouse. Gonzales noticed Kane's look and whispered:

'Lago's girl. No trespassing!'

As the girl passed the bar she noticed Kane. A smile appeared on the full lips.

'Bueno, Gonzales,' she said. 'Who is this handsome hombre?'

'Oh . . . a visitor.'

'Hey, Zita,' Babe Lago shouted. 'Come here.'

She ignored him. She stopped beside Kane and smiled up at him. The tip of her tongue darted out teasingly. 'I'm called Zita, senor,' she said invitingly.

'Kane, senorita.'

Gonzales waved her away impatiently. The door creaked as Clay Sanderson entered. Without saying anything he leaned his back against the wall and studied Zita with interest.

'Zita!' Lago shouted again.

'He shouted for you,' Kane said.

She leaned forward. He could see her breasts in the low-cut, wide blouse.

'He doesn't shout loud enough, Senor Kane! You only need to whisper . . . Zita will hear, and obey.' Once again the red tip of her tongue slid along the full lips. 'Will you whisper to me? Whisper to me!' She was so near that Kane could feel the warmth from her.

With a crash a chair fell down. Kane half-turned. Babe Lago stood crouched, his green eyes glowing strangely.

'Keep away from her, Kane!' he sneered. 'I got my own brand on her.'

Kane's eyes narrowed.

'I don't see any brand,' he answered quietly.

'Then you take a good look!' Lago bellowed, his right hand hovering nervously over his revolver.

Zita moved a few paces away from Kane. Out of the corner of his eye he could see that Clay Sanderson had straightened up.

Kane said: 'You just watching, Sanderson?'

'Sure. I'm out of this one.'

Zita shouted, 'Don't try to be a man, Babe! A puppy has to learn to bark before he can bite!'

Bitch, Kane thought, why doesn't she shut her damned mouth! He saw that it was just a question of seconds before

Lago's tense muscles relaxed again. He stared at the gunman's eyes. They were deep in concentration. A twitch of the body told him that the hand was on its way to the revolver. Everything happened so fast that nobody in the room could follow it.

Kane's Colt 'Police' Special roared twice, so fast that the shots sounded as one. Lago's weapon swung loosely in the paralysed right hand, he fell backwards against the wall, swung around and dropped the revolver on to the floor. With both hands against the wall he tried to stay upright. Then the stiff, dead body relaxed and he sank slowly to his knees, slid over on to his side and fell across the shining, polished revolver.

Kane lowered his gun. His eyes distant and bitter. He turned to the bar. Gonzales looked at him with his mouth gaping. Zita moved slowly away. Kane looked at her.

'Get the hell outa here, you . . . !'

She rushed out.

Clay Sanderson came over to the bar. He grabbed a bottle and filled two glasses. Without saying anything he pushed one towards Kane. Kane emptied it. He looked at his hands. They were as steady as a rock.

Sanderson said quietly, 'I wouldn't lose sleep over Babe Lago, if I were you. He was just a creep!'

'Thanks for the drink,' Kane answered and turned to go.

Gonzales said nothing. Sanderson threw a couple of coins on to the bar and followed Kane out into the dark street. Kane heard his footsteps and turned.

'Still staying out of the fun, Sanderson?' he said threateningly.

'You bet. Wait a minute, Kane.' He came over to Kane and followed him over to the hitching post. 'I'd like to ask you a question,' he said quietly. 'You don't need to answer if you're not interested. Okay?'

'Okay.' Kane loosened the reins and the black stallion moved in anticipation.

'You in Mexico to earn a quick dollar?'

'Sure.'

'Interested in earning a hundred times what Don Marco's paying you?'

Kane felt a jolt to his nervous system. 'What do you know about Don Marco, Saderson?' he asked quietly.

'Rumours are flying along the border these days,' Sanderson answered dryly. 'Didn't take us long to hear how you were pushed out of El Paso by the sheriff there. We also found out that you're a revolvèro for Don Marco.'

'You're talking in the plural all the time,' Kane said. 'Who are we?'

'Some friends of mine.'

'If you know so much then you also know that the job's a cinch,' Kane said casually. 'Food's good, the wine's free and the pay's great.'

'How much would you risk for ... let's say twenty thousand dollars, Kane?'

Kane didn't answer immediately. He laughed. 'My life, I guess,' he said. His heart was beating heavily in his chest now.

'Come back tomorrow night,' Sanderson said quietly. 'Think it over. And I don't need to say that you'd better keep this to yourself?'

Kane chuckled. 'I'm kind-hearted,' he said, 'but not when it concerns twenty thousand—or my life.'

'All right,' Sanderson said, turning to go. 'See that hut over there? I'll be there at ten tomorrow evening.'

He disappeared into the darkness. Kane heard muffled hoof beats that slowly died away. He ached to follow him but checked himself. It wouldn't be wise to do anything silly now. They had offered him the bait, all he had to do was to take it gently and let the fisherman or fishermen decide what to do then. Kane had no doubt that Clay Sanderson was one of 'the whipped ones.' He was also sure that Babe Lago had been a needle eye that he had had to pass through. He was also willing to bet his last cent that Zita had been an important part of the puzzle. She had teased Lago to make him draw on Kane. Kane was so sure about it that he couldn't be bothered to visit her and beat the truth out of her.

Well, 'the whipped ones' had put him to the test—and seemed satisfied. Kane was full of expectancy. They must have kept a close watch on him, and had great respect for his abilities. Or maybe they'd really try him now. He'd know by tomorrow evening anyway. He mounted and rode slowly back to the hacienda.

CHAPTER EIGHT

Kane could see light coming from the hut as he neared it the following evening. He could hear the clink of glasses and howls of laughter coming from the cantina. A coyote howled from a ridge north of town. Kane had his right hand on his revolver and led the horse behind him with his left.

The door was badly made and hardly filled the frame.

'Hello,' he said quietly. 'Sanderson?'

He stood to one side of the door—in deep shadow—and the Colt was in his hand now.

He heard footsteps and the door was suddenly opened.

'Kane?' It was Sanderson.

'Yeah.'

'Come in. And for God's sake put that gun away.'

Kane smiled at Sanderson's nervous tone of voice.

He threw the reins over a hitching post and went inside. It was just an adobe hut with earthern floor, simple furniture and smoking oil lamps. On the table stood a bottle of tequila and two glasses. Sanderson was unarmed.

'Drink?'

'No thanks,' Kane answered. He studied Sanderson in the dim light. The sun-burned flecks on his face had almost disappeared.

'Spit it out,' Kane said. 'I ain't got all night.'

'All right. The boss wants to talk to you. He's got a proposition for you.'

'About what?'

'I've no idea.'

'What're you in all this?'

'I was told to contact you,' Sanderson answered. 'The boss told me to tell you that you had nothing to fear. This is not a trap. He just wants to talk to you, offer you a deal and let you go if you're not interested.'

The last remark didn't ring quite right to Kane's ears. He knew that 'the whipped ones' couldn't make him an offer and then let him go if he refused. They'd never let a man go who knew the slightest thing about them. It was a primitive sort of trap and Kane was disappointed in them. He had expected more—something more artistic.

'All right,' he said.

'It's some distance to ride. I've got my horse at the back of this hut.'

Kane turned towards the door. 'Let's blow then.'

As soon as he went out into the darkness he knew he had made a mistake. The muffled clicks in the darkness behind him confirmed what Sanderson said,

'Just stand real quiet, Kane.'

The revolver was torn out of his holster. When his night vision returned Kane saw three figures standing by his horse. Not artistic enough, eh? he said mockingly to himself.

'The boss is a careful man,' Sanderson went on. 'He wants us to tie you up. You agree to it or do we have to knock you senseless and tie you to the saddle?'

Kane worked out the distance and angle of the shots towards the three figures. It was hopeless. He shrugged. 'What're you thinking of using—a branding iron?'

'A *bandana* will do, Kane.'

A scarf was put over his eyes and bound tightly at the back of his neck. A strong hand gripped his arm.

'This way.'

They led him over to the stallion and he mounted. He knew that a sudden jab with the spurs would make the stallion shoot off like a bullet and he'd stand a good chance of getting away. He would have done so if the circumstances had been different but he wanted to talk to this

'Boss' they mentioned—the boss of the Flagellados. He decided to obey every order they gave him like a well-trained dog.

The saddles creaked and a couple of horses snorted.

'Let's go,' he heard Sanderson say.

Kane judged that the trip took a couple of hours. He was completely blind the whole time but he could still form a mental picture of the landscape they rode through. First he had the wind from the left the whole time. That meant that they kept a steady course to the north. Secondly, the sound of the hoofs on rock told him that they had left the grassy stretches. That meant that they were riding upwards, up the slopes of a smaller mountain range, a branch of the mightier Sierra Nevada. Thirdly Kane heard water rushing on his right-hand side during the trip, which was a characteristic sound of a river that was fast-flowing. That also confirmed his ideas that they were high up.

Suddenly he heard dogs barking and voices. Sanderson shouted something in Spanish.

They rode on, then the horse stopped. The bandana was taken off and Kane blinked in the light of torches. When his vision returned to normal he saw a low, long stone building that lay beneath a dark mountain crest. The house lay on a kind of shelf, covered by long grass, cholla and mesquite. On the lower side of the shelf or ledge Kane could make out a dark abyss. Judging by the echoes of the voices it must be quite a drop, by the sound of it, Kane thought. He saw at least eight men dressed in white in front of the house. When he turned in the saddle he could see the narrow path just outside the range of light. He shuddered. The thought that he had ridden up that narrow, winding goat track blind-folded was frightening. One false step on the horse's part and he would have plunged over the edge. Kane patted the horse's neck.

'Dismount,' Sanderson said.

Two Mexicans—or half-breeds—took the horses. Kane followed Sanderson over the clearing towards the house. When he came closer he could see that it was certainly no ordinary herdsman's cottage. It looked more like a hacienda —long, low and built in a U-shape. The walls were of solid stone and the shutters were of iron-studded cedar.

Sanderson opened the heavy door and let Kane go in first. They came into a large, open hall. The floor was paved and in one corner an open fire cast light over the rough stone walls, skins and blankets that hung there. Sanderson pointed to a door at the end of the hall. Kane moved towards it. He could hear his escort behind him. He knew that they kept their guns on him the whole time.

Sanderson knocked on the next door, opened it and let Kane go in first.

It was a big room, surprisingly big. There was a group of men in the room, most of them white, the rest a mixture of Mexicans, Pueblo Indians and half-breeds. Everyone was dressed in magnificent Mexican suits and heavily armed. At a table in the middle of the room sat a small, fat man in a gold-embroidered suit. His cravat was of snow-white silk and a nut-sized ruby glowed in the silk. His short, stubby fingers were covered in flashing rings. His shoulders were enormous and in the well-tailored jacket he looked almost square in proportion. His head was large, round and completely hairless. His ears were small and disformed. He had no neck at all, his head giving the impression that it had been screwed down into the unnaturally broad shoulders. His nose was flat, with large, dark nostrils. Kane had the impression that he could see right into his head. His mouth was small and narrow—like a slit in his face. But his eyes didn't seem to fit the clown-like surrounding features—they were big, almond shaped and bore a cold, direct look that came as a physical shock. When Kane met the eyes he felt no desire to smile.

'Senor Kane,' the man said politely. 'Please sit down.' He pointed to a high-backed chair in front of his desk.

Kane sat down.

'You may call me El Fiero,' the man said. 'I've been known by that name for years and it is just as good as any other.'

El Fiero, Kane thought, automatically translating the name to 'the terrible' or the 'terrifying one'. He thought the name was suitable for this character resembling both clown and devil.

'I won't tire you with introductions to my companions,' El Fiero said in fluent English, 'and anyway, their names would mean nothing to you.'

Kane decided to take the offensive immediately. 'Get to the point,' he said briefly. 'I ain't got all the time in the world.'

El Fiero's eyes filmed in anger. He said slowly and clearly:

'I presume your American manner of speech and ignorance of who I am is the reason for your disrespectful and shameful conduct. But for your own good I suggest you do not repeat it. I am the absolute monarch here in the "Eagles' Nest" and you are in my power completely. It would take no more than twenty seconds to remove your tongue, Senor Kane!'

'Sanderson talked about a deal you had to offer,' Kane said coldly. 'Do you want the answer signalled or do I keep my tongue until I can tell you what I think of it?'

El Fiero studied him for some time. Kane's slate-grey eyes never flinched a fraction. An approving look crossed El Fiero's face.

'I appreciate personal courage, Senor Kane. But stubbornness and obstinacy is often exchanged for it. The reports from Encinillas say that you have courage and also a touch of the latter. Your ability with a gun meets with my approval. I will now give you five minutes to decide whether you are interested in what I have to offer. Ready?'

Kane nodded.

'Let me add first that I wish no protests while I explain the facts. You're called Morgan Kane. You are not wanted in Texas but the sheriffs in El Paso and Laredo have had an eye on you recently. You were pushed out of El Paso after making trouble at the gaming tables. You crossed Rio Bravo hunting for easily earned money, thinking of the threat from the Flagellados. You are not the first who have offered rich ranchers their guns for hire. Enough of that, Don Marco hired you for four hundred pesos a month. Your job is to shadow his daughter on her trips around the hacienda, trips that she seems to insist on making with youthful stubbornness. How you came into contact with Don Marco we don't know, but we'll find out—if it's necessary.'

Zachary will fix that too, Kane thought, thinking of his colleague and the job he had done along the border.

'Don Marco is afraid the Flagellados will steal his daughter and demand a ransom that will ruin him. He knows that he'll pay what is demanded for Marguerita and he knows that we will demand a sum that for him will come to three hundred and fifty thousand silver pesos. It would ruin him completely.'

Kane said nothing. He noticed something that was leaning against El Fiero's chair. His thoughts went back to the scars he had had described for him on the dead bandits. Was that why they called him El Fiero—'The terrible one'?

El Fiero noticed his glance. 'I'll come back to this Sabadilla later. At the moment I wish to have your full attention.' His eyes once again seemed to be covered by a green film and Kane began to wonder if El Fiero was on the verge of insanity.

'We are offering you fifty thousand silver pesos to get Don Marco's daughter to a special place and turn her over to us, Senor Kane.'

'I'll do it for seventy five thousand.'

The room was deathly quiet. It seemed that the others there daren't breathe. Kane realised that this must be the first time that anyone had dared oppose El Fiero. He sat there, unflinching, staring at the eyes in front of him. The greenish film was clearly seen now.

'I'm not sure if this is some form of courage—or stupid obstinacy,' El Fiero said quietly, almost in a friendly tone.

'Neither,' Kane answered. 'It's a risky job and worth the money. I value my life at seventy-five thousand pesos, Fiero. I find that pretty cheap compared to what Senorita Marguerita is worth.'

El Fiero's small mouth opened in a silent chuckle.

'Bravo, Senor Kane—that explanation just saved your life! Bueno, then you shall have seventy-five thousand. You accept the deal?'

'Of course.'

'Why of course, senor?' The voice seemed to creep around Kane.

'I like money. A lot of money. A man gets tired of playing with cards up his sleeve for grub money. And anyway, I don't feel like investigating the cliff just outside the house. I guess that I'd end up down there if I said no?'

'Very smart, Senor Kane! But don't believe that a simple yes will make you bullet-proof. We cannot follow you back and check on you, but I presume that you know you will never leave Mexico alive if you betray us.' The slash of a mouth smiled horribly. 'You will in that case realise that the Flagellados have eyes all along the border—and we know how to treat traitors. A little later I'll give you proof of it.'

El Fiero leaned forward in his chair. His almond-shaped eyes shone.

'In three days, senor ... you ride out with the senorita. You suggest that you ride north to Buenaventura. You ride along the Santa Clara. At a place along the river you'll find us. That's all.'

Kane said:

'That's much, much farther than she usually rides. What if she is suspicious or protests?'

'Seventy-five thousand pesos, Senor Kane. THAT problem is yours, getting her there. And please don't disappoint us.'

'Okay. When? What time of day?'

'Any time.'

'Okay. And the money?'

'You'll get it in silver when she is delivered.'

Yeah, Kane thought, and a bullet in the back... But loudly he answered, 'Seems okay to me.'

El Fiero got up. He couldn't have been more than five feet tall at the most. With his enormous upper part of the body he looked as if he had no legs. Kane realised that El Fiero was born like that, a cripple.

'I promised you a demonstration of how we treat traitors,' El Fiero said. 'A man whom we placed in a hacienda farther north told of our plans. Diego! Fetch him.'

One of the half-breeds bowed and disappeared. El Fiero took the whip and weighed it in his hand. 'A Sabadilla,' he said mildly. 'It is nine and half foot long. Its weight is four pounds. Its tail is three plaited strips liberally studded with octagonal silver pieces. I have found that it is most effective. The handle is bound with thin strips of stag skin. Inside it is made of hickory, strengthened with a piece of iron near the grip. The tail is made of mule-skin, with a special heavy sort of grass woven in. Pay heed to the flexible joint between the handle and tail. Senor, you have heard of other famous whips, the known "jambok" for example, that is made of the sexual organs of the ox, stretched and dried in the sun. I assure you, senor, the Spanish Sabadilla is just as effective.'

The door opened and a man was pushed in, his hands bound behind his back—he was half-naked and had chains on his feet. Kane noticed that the man was white.

'His name means nothing,' El Fiero said as the wretched creature was dragged over to the wall and chained with his back to the room. A couple of men fetched some grass mats and placed them under him.

'I have no wish to make a mess on the floor,' El Fiero explained. 'Blood has a tendency to attract flies and I despise insects.' He looked at the man with his face to the wall.

'Is he ready, Diego? Fine. I would like to have your full attention now, Mr Kane.'

El Fiero took off his jacket. Kane stared. What he first thought was fat turned out to be muscles, unnatural muscles, so enormous that the white, silk shirt almost tore across the back as he gripped the whip and tested it a couple of times.

'Twenty lashes should be enough, it usually is, Senor Kane. Would you mind counting—loudly?'

El Fiero stood with legs astride and let the whip run across the floor, then he drew back his right shoulder and threw his arm with terrible force. With a dull smack the whip lashed the naked back and a shower of blood flecked the grass mats.

Kane swallowed. 'One,' he said.

The man was still conscious until the eleventh lash.

'Twenty,' Kane said, hoarsely.

El Fiero turned and gave the dripping whip to one of the half-breeds. 'Not too much fat, Diego, or it'll be too soft.' He looked at Kane's pale face and narrow, glittering eyes. 'I see that you are impressed, senor. You have reason to be. There is only one other man in Mexico that can use the Sabadilla like I do. You are sweating, senor? Too warm for you, perhaps? Diego, open a window. We mustn't forget that Senor Kane—capable as he is—is still just a gringo. Now, can I offer you a glass of wine, Senor Kane?'

'No,' Kane managed to say, nausea stuck like a lump in his throat. The remains of the man was still hanging in the chains on the wall.

El Fiero raised his hand. 'Remove him.' He put on his jacket and sat down.

'Well, senor,' he continued, 'I look forward to meeting you here again—in a couple of days. I never leave this house, you see. And remember, senor—just the senorita and yourself. You are not so stupid as to believe that you can perhaps make a trap for us?'

'No.'

'Good. Sanderson will lead you back to Encinillas in the same way as you came here. I look forward to seeing you again, Senor Kane.'

'The same here, Senor Fiero.'

He was put on his horse again, his eyes were covered and he sat deep in thought during the two to three hours ride back. His thoughts were chaotic. Could he contact Zachary in some way, who must also contact La Guardia Civil—the

Mexican civil guard? Would it be possible for them to surround the district somehow? Could he find the place again in daylight? Or would an appeal to the authorities be received with just polite, doubting smiles and shrugs? Most likely. A ride through the dark. A cripple. A big house. A whip. A fantastic sum of money. Imagination? Too much tequila?

Kane felt sick. Should he tell Don Marco the whole story? Sure, and then what would happen. Rita would never leave the house. If necessary her father would lock her in. Her life would be saved, sure—but what kind of life? And he remembered what Fiero had said: 'A man farther north whom we had placed on a hacienda...' How did they get hold of him? How did they get him out from the hacienda? The answer was there. The Flagellados had their spies inside the walls—most likely also in Don Marco's hacienda! Two hundred vaqueros. Any one of them might belong to the Flagellados. He—Kane—would be watched continually. The least sign of betrayal ... well ... he couldn't stay awake for ever—and certainly not spend the rest of his life under the protection of Don Marco.

He moved uneasily in the saddle. What in hell was he going to do? Take her with him—deliver her to El Fiero? What would they do to her? Violate her? Or just hold her there until her father paid up? Three other girls had been released by the Flagellados. He hadn't heard if any of them had been touched in any way. But could he take such a risk? Could he hope to free her, kill El Fiero and a lot of his men before biting the dust himself? Was this the only way one could come up to the 'Eagles' Nest'? Kane found no answer to his problems. He knew that he'd have to do this alone, taking full responsibility. Shane, Don Marco, they'd all have refused him.

Kane found that he had two alternatives. To warn Don Marco, something that would lead to Rita being locked in for years—or until she managed to escape in desperation. That would mean he wouldn't be needed on the hacienda. That would also mean that 'the whipped ones' would be after him from the moment he walked outside the hacienda. And he didn't doubt that they could take him whenever they wanted to—their organisation worked very effectively.

The other alternative was to follow the game through, get Rita to Santa Clara, take the chance that El Fiero had use for him and hope to burn down the whole of the 'Eagles' Nest'. In Kane's reasoning there lay an intense wish for a hero's death. He was fairly sure that El Fiero hadn't checked on him in detail just to leave him with a bullet in the back at Santa Clara. There was more to it than that and Kane was willing to take a chance on it. He suddenly realised that he had made a decision. His doubts left him. There was no way back now. To think of what Shane would say was ridiculous. If this didn't work out he wouldn't stay alive anyway. And if he made it—well, only time would tell. He had Shane's word that this was his mission and he could do it the way he wanted to. Okay, from now on I'm a member of the Flagellados...

They took off the scarf outside Encinillas, gave him his revolver back and disappeared into the darkness. Kane felt like following them again but he had a feeling that he was being watched so he dropped the idea. He started back south to the hacienda. He sat with head bowed in the saddle. It started to turn red in the eastern sky. Kane's eyes were narrowed in concentration. He could still see the man hanging in the chains. He felt a terrible hatred for the monster up there in the 'Eagles' Nest'.

The sun peeped over Conchos Mountain as Kane rode into the hacienda. A beautiful white cockerel stood on top of a heap of manure and flapped its wings. It crowed at the sun.

Kane dismounted. The stable boys ran up. He threw the reins down and longed desperately for a drink and a bed. The cock crowed again.

CHAPTER NINE

'I married him,' Cathy Taylor said quietly, 'and that was the biggest mistake of my life. I should have known that an alcoholic can't change his ways. I managed it for three years, washed and ironed for people, sewed and looked after children, and he drank up everything. When he died I just felt relief. I moved from town and headed west, knowing that there was always a demand for teachers in the settler stretches out west. I've taught kids their alphabets and multiplication tables and the Our Father and about Lincoln and Louis the fourteenth, from Cincinatti to El Paso—and I've enjoyed it immensely.'

Insects sang in the trees above them. The garden was dark and quiet in front of the patio. Kane took a drag of his cigarette. The sudden glow accentuated the dark hollows of his eyes and the hard lines around his mouth.

'And you ended in Mexico,' he said dryly.

'Yes. I was offered the job while I was in El Paso. I was a governess at two haciendas before coming here. I love Mexico. The people are friendly and kind. There is peace and quiet here.' She glanced at him. 'You're smiling, Morgan. Yes, peace and quiet mean starvation for you and your type.'

There was sadness in her voice. Kane took another drag of his cigarette.

'This hacienda is a world in itself,' she went on, dreamily. 'Here I can sit and dream, just dream. And listen. Someday you'll maybe understand what that means for a person.'

'When I get tired of killing people, you mean?' he said

brutally, annoyed with her quiet manner and naïvety.

'I didn't say that. But you live with trouble, Morgan. You're a man that may have this restlessness in his blood but sooner or later a person must stop looking for what lies on the other side of the hill. I did that, I looked *back*, looked at my life and found that it was poor, meaningless, worthless.'

Kane suddenly had the urge to tear her out of her self-satisfied dream, to hurt her, maybe because her words touched on something inside himself.

'Some would call that escapism, Cathy. One can always take on a peaceful, light, easy job. I knew a man who after eight years as a marshal changed his job. He found peace and quiet and time to dream. He settled in the south of Mexico as a cobbler. Nobody shot at him there. Nobody shoots cobblers.'

'You're cold, Morgan! You respect only violence and that strength is right!'

She sat there for a while without speaking.

'You know what,' she said quietly, 'I feel sorry for you. Capable in your work as you are, you lack something—warmth. You live your own, egoistical life. Everything is to be used and made use of by Morgan Kane. Maybe you'll end up rich by your work—but you'll always remain poor, because you use the wrong measure to judge by, you use money.'

'You're getting too self-assured, Cathy,' he said quickly. 'It was money your husband drank up that finished you—and your marriage. It's easy to look down on money when one's sitting high and dry and knows that one has a roof over one's head the following day and from then on.'

'You don't have to tell me, I know that! I know better than most! But you don't understand what I'm trying to say, Morgan—you'll never understand. You are as you are, are made like that and will STAY like that. It's not so hard to understand, maybe.'

Kane lit another cigarette. He didn't like this at all. He hated being lectured to and especially dissected. Even though he was only half-listening to what was being said, hardly taking it all in—the words rang a bell and depressed him. Maybe she was right. Maybe he was cold and hard—lacking human feelings.

He took a sip from his glass. The liquor warmed him and to think of something else he began to look at her as a woman, a sexual object. And in the back of his mind something hammered and hammered, next day ... next day ... next day ...

The pale light from the lamp threw an enticing glow around her golden head. Her mouth was soft, showing sensual lines that deep inside he knew weren't there, but he wanted to see them, to be attracted by them to release some of the pressure inside him.

'What are you thinking of?' she suddenly asked.

'You.'

She laughed. 'I thought it was Rita who filled your thoughts, not an ageing governess, with a sad life behind her.'

'You're no more than thirty, Cathy.'

'Twenty-nine.'

He chuckled.

She didn't drop the subject. 'Do you often think of Rita?'

'How do you mean?'

'It wouldn't be surprising. She's the loveliest girl in Chihuahua.'

Kane stifled a yawn. 'Is she?'

She gathered her shawl around her. It was suddenly cold. 'It's late,' she said, nervously. 'I think I'll go to bed. Good night.'

'Good night, Cathy.'

She turned when she was up on the patio. He could see her silhouette and felt suddenly lonely.

'What about you?'

'I'll ... I'll just sit for a while longer.'

'Well ... good night.' The door closed behind her. A little later he heard another door close somewhere inside the dark, sleeping house.

He leaned back in his chair and tried to convince himself that he didn't give a damn. He had cigarettes, liquor and a warm, quiet night. Plenty of time, time to wait. For what? Damn it all! He crushed the cigarette, emptied the glass and started to walk back through the garden. He glanced up at Rita's window as he passed. He was startled. The window was open and on the small balcony that was overgrown with ivy he could make out a white figure against the black door opening.

Her voice reached down to him.

'Well, senor ... has she left you now?'

He stood and looked up at her. There was something exciting about the scene, the dark garden, the smell of flowers, the balcony and the girl in the mist-like night-dress. His heart beat with a heavy, numbing rhythm at the thought of her—and El Fiero. He tried to think of something to say—something stupid, without meaning, something that would make her laugh. He suddenly wanted her to laugh. He suddenly thought of El Fiero's slit of a mouth and its silent chuckle. He swallowed and turned to go.

'Kane!'

He turned.

'Don't go ...'

In a second she had thrown one leg over the balustrade and was climbing down. It wasn't more than nine feet yet he stood gasping when he saw the thin silk billow up around her naked, beautiful legs. Then he came to his senses and he was suddenly furious. In three strides he was over by her. He gripped her shoulders and hissed,

'Are you crazy, Rita? Get up there again!'

An intoxicating odour filled his nostrils, from her body, from the gully between her breasts, from her hair that hung loosely down her back—and his hands on the naked shoulders suddenly felt feverish and clammy. The starlight shone in her eyes. She raised her face to him, slowly, slowly and he felt desire rushing through him like a torrent.

'Kane,' she whispered gently. 'Oh, Kane ...'

His resistance fell apart then. He pulled her against him

so brutally that she moaned, then her mouth was over his and the stars, trees, house—all collapsed in a wild dance before his eyes. He could feel her nails in his neck, it was a wonderful pain—he felt her teeth pressing against his lips giving him a delightful pain, he felt the desire welling up in his body, heard her heavy sighs against his cheek, felt her body grow soft and heavy, burning with desire—he just wanted to lay her down and make love to her, hard and gentle, quick but make it last ... then a night bird screamed from a tree. He came to his senses, saw the house, trees, stars, felt her skin prickle in the night air, felt his own spit on his cheek and the passion left him, leaving only an empty, gnawing feeling in its place—like the after-effects of a dream.

'Go up,' he mumbled. 'You hear ... get back up there ...'

'But ... but ...'

'Git!' he said, brutally. El Fiero's smile leered before his eyes. 'Go on ... go!' Her tears annoyed him—made him angry. What in hell was she crying for?

'Go, Rita!'

He turned and walked away between the trees. Her muffled crying followed him. If only she would stop! Why —why did this have to happen? Now ... with just a few hours before ... before EL FIERO!

He thought of the jar of tequila in his hut. He walked faster—almost running. Gasping for breath he stood in the dark hut. The jar was chilled, cold against the palm of his hand. He bit out the cork with his teeth. The smell of the liquor filled his nostrils. He put the jar down. He daren't drink tonight—not tonight. He put the cork back in place. The night bird screamed again—as if he was being beaten with the Sabadilla.

CHAPTER TEN

Early the following morning he lay on his bed and went over his plans. The day before he had asked Don Marco to send one of his most trusted vaqueros to the nearest telegraph office to send a telegraph to Zachary in El Paso. In the telegraph Kane informed Zachary that he had made contact with 'the whipped ones' and had asked him to come to Encinillas. Kane said no more, knowing that his colleague would read between the lines and understand that Kane needed help. Afterwards he had studied a map of Chihuahua and remembering all the impressions his senses had received during the trip up to the 'Eagles' Nest' he could more or less place where the house lay—maybe a few miles give or take in each direction. It was the river that helped him most. He had found out that it was the Rio Carmen that flowed through the heights north of Encinillas and formed water-falls at various points.

Kane felt calm, relaxed. The knowledge that Zachary was on his way to Encinillas steadied his nerves. Zachary knew as much about 'the whipped ones' as Kane did and had enough imagination to realise that Encinillas was the end of the line. Kane had wondered if he should ask Zachary to gather a large posse and ride north but gave up the idea. 'The whipped ones' would certainly be keeping a wary eye open, just in case Kane betrayed them and a mistake like that would mean the death of him and Rita.

Somebody knocked on the door and a servant girl brought his breakfast, flap-jacks, jam and coffee. There was also a bowl full of fruit. Kane emptied the coffee pot but didn't touch the fruit.

When he strolled out the sun was already above Conchos Mountain. He went up to the hacienda and waved to one of the servants.

'Ask the senorita if she'd like to take a ride this morning.'

'Si, senor.'

He lit a cigarette and waited impatiently for her. The servant appeared a little later. He seemed disturbed.

'The senorita apologises—she is not feeling well.'

Kane cursed inwardly. 'Is she in her room?'

'Si, senor.'

Kane nodded to the servant and wandered through the garden towards the west wing where her room was. He saw that the large windows stood open.

'Rita,' he shouted, quietly. 'Rita!'

No answer.

Kane picked up a pebble and threw it at her window. It made quite a loud noise.

'Rita!'

Her head appeared.

'Come out,' he said. 'I've got to talk to you.'

'I have nothing to say to you, senor.' Her face was unnaturally pale against the black hair.

'I'm sorry for what happened yesterday,' he said quietly. 'Please come and take a ride with me before it gets too warm. I must talk to you. It's important.'

Her face took on more colour. He could see that she was dressed in trousers and a blouse.

'What do you want to say, senor?'

'Damn it, I can't stand here and say it,' he said angrily. 'Don't act like a kid. Get your riding clothes on and I'll ask the stable boys to get the horses ready.'

She was still uncertain.

'Hurry!' he said impatiently.

A smile appeared on her face. She turned and disappeared.

Kane breathed a sigh of relief and went down to the stables. He asked for Diablo Blanco and Diablo del Notte to be saddled up. Then he went back to the adobe and packed a few odds and ends in his saddle bag. He took a short-barrelled carbine, filled a water-bottle with water and went back.

Rita came hurrying out, a white ribbon shining in her dark hair. She was dressed the same as she was on their first trip—all in black.

The stable boys waved to them as they rode out. Kane felt that the smile he gave her was too strained but it didn't look as if she noticed it. She stood in the stirrups and took a deep breath of air.

'Let's ride, Morgan—fast!' she shouted.

'Okay.'

The white and black horses galloped side by side over the green, rolling plains.

A mile or so from the hacienda they reined in the horses and continued at a trot. Kane noticed that she was looking at him but he said nothing.

'You seem worried,' she said with a smile. 'Is what happened yesterday bothering you?' The smile was a challenge but he paid no heed to it.

'Maybe. You're dangerously attractive, Rita.'

'Am I?' She laughed, gayly. 'Do you know what, Morgan—you're the first man who has ever made me feel that ... well, that I'm attractive and desirable. Earlier, I've only felt tied down, forced to do everything, as if I was just a valuable object. But now!' She threw out her arms and seemed to envelope the mountains, plains and the clear air. 'Now I feel free. I feel like a woman! Do you understand what I'm trying to say? No, I doubt it—freedom is something you take for granted.'

'Maybe.'

She pulled the white mare nearer his stallion.

'Have you always been a ... revolvèro, Morgan?'

'Not always.'

'What did you do before then?'

'Oh ... trapper, cattle-driver, prospector for gold, gambler. A bit of each. Can't we head north? I've never ridden there before.'

She nodded. They began to ride northwards. Kane felt his stomach turn over. His eyes flashed to and fro from under the brim of his hat. When he turned in the saddle he saw that the hacienda had disappeared behind a low ridge. How far had they ridden—three, four miles?

'You must have experienced quite a lot,' she said. 'I envy you all your adventures, your experiences, everything you've seen and heard. Mexican women are the country's last slaves—are you aware of that? But there'll be a change here one day. Just wait!'

He said nothing.

She looked around. 'We've never ridden this far before.'

'Afraid?' he asked.

Her eyes met his. 'I'm never afraid of anything when I'm with you,' she said softly.

He forced himself to smile. 'It's lovely here. Is there a river over there?'

She nodded. 'The Santa Clara. But it's quite a way there. Must be about three hours' riding.'

Three hours! Kane clenched his teeth. Christ, was it so far away!

'Been there before?'

'When I was smaller.'

'Is it pretty there?'

'Yes, beautiful.'

He looked at her. 'Shall we ride there?'

'Father has forbidden me to ride so far, even with you.'

He bent down and patted the horse on the neck. 'If we had been riding good horses instead of these nags...'

Her eyes lit up. 'Let's go! We can bathe there!' Like a flash the white mare flew past Kane. He spurred the stallion and chased after her. They rode through a couple of long, ridges covered in undergrowth and followed a valley northwards. The sinking feeling in Kane's stomach got slowly worse. Then the valley opened out. In a large, open clearing he saw a couple of stags dodge away, terrified.

She pointed across the plain ahead. 'The river's over there!'

'Take it easy,' he said. 'We've got plenty of time.'

He had a wild urge to grab her horse and head back at speed to the hacienda and safety.

They spent over an hour crossing the plain. On their left they had the foothills of the Sierra Nevada, blue and hazy in the distance. Rita loosened the silk scarf she wore around her neck.

'Madre Dios, it's warm,' she sighed. 'It will be wonderful to bathe. Are you shy, Kane? There is only one bathing spot that is big enough.' Her laughter was free, joyful and under other circumstances he would have felt excited but now he was uneasy, doubtful and hated himself for what he was doing.

'We can take it in turns to bathe,' he said.

She laughed again.

On the other side of the plain it sloped down towards the valley floor where the Santa Clara meandered lazily. Unlike other Mexican rivers this one was clear and clean.

She pointed to a spot, a pool that an earlier avalanche had made.

'That's where we used to bathe!' She looked at him. 'Are you afraid, Morgan? Of me ... or the Flagellados?'

He had to fight to look calm. 'On this horse I'm not afraid of anyone.'

They rode quickly down the slope. She jumped off and ran towards the bank. She pulled off her boot and sock and dipped her foot in the water.

'The water is lovely! Come on, Kane, hurry and take off your clothes!'

'I'll wait until you're finished,' he said calmly. 'I'll sit here and take a smoke. So just dive in! I won't peep!'

'GRINGO!' she shouted teasingly and started to undo her shirt.

Kane sat with his right side to her. He rolled a cigarette and looked carefully down the river. Dense bushes and a few trees grew along the bank. It was the same in the other direction too. The slope on the other side of the pool had the same type of undergrowth and a few scattered pines.

He couldn't help seeing her standing there with her hands over her head, tying up her hair in a knot. She must have known that he was watching her. She stood still as she tied up her hair. She was slim, golden and beautiful. Kane's stomach knotted at the thought of what could happen to her lovely body. He was also painfully aware that she was doing this, showing herself to him, giving herself to him without reservation, because she trusted him, liked him ... maybe was in love with him.

She turned. She didn't scream, didn't try to hide herself, just stood there and looked at him. Kane's heart beat slowly and heavily.

'Come,' she said, lifting her arm to Kane. 'Come, Morgan!'

Four men burst out of the undergrowth on the other side of the pool, twenty yards from Rita—forty yards from Kane. They just stood there—their rifles at the ready.

'Come on then,' she shouted. 'Come on!'

A man roared with laughter behind her.

She whirled around and crouched down immediately. Her voice shrieked with fear.

'Senor Kane!' a voice shouted. 'Get some clothes on her and go back to the horses. Well done, amigo!'

Kane fetched her clothes and went down to her with them. She had turned her back on the men—a poor attempt to hide herself from the staring eyes.

'Morgan,' she whispered. '... are they ... are they ...?'

'Yes,' he answered. 'Flagellados.'

She grabbed him by the shoulders, her golden breasts almost touching his chest. Her eyes were filled with fear and desperation.

'Amigo ... they called you amigo!'

Something splashed in the pool.

'Get dressed!' Kane snapped. She pulled her shirt and trousers on. Kane didn't turn around. He heard hoof beats from all directions. They came from all sides.

'Morgan,' she sobbed in fear. 'Say you're not ... say ... Madre Dios ...'

'I'm one of them, Rita. But listen ... later ... when ...'

A hand swung Kane around.

Clay Sanderson smiled at him.

'El Fiero is impatient,' he said dryly. Kane felt his revolver taken away by someone behind him. He glanced at Rita. She suddenly seemed small and grey. Her face was white, deathly pale—it was as if her spark of life had left her. Kane realised now how shocked she must be. To be seen naked together with a gringo, by the Flagellados! And then learn—or believe—that *he* was one of them and had arranged the whole thing, betrayed her love, youth, beauty ...!

Kane's eyes narrowed. Sanderson let go his shoulder and backed away.

'Easy, amigo,' he hissed. 'Let's ride.'

They had to lift Rita into the saddle. She was apathetic, almost paralysed. Kane watched her nervously. There were nine riders, who kept the horses between them. They rode over the river and up the bank on the other side. Then they swung sharply to the north-east and followed almost invisible animal tracks upwards, up the rocky mountain slopes. At one spot the path was so narrow that they had to ride after each other. On the right the mountain wall towered above them, on their left a cliff which dropped a hundred and fifty feet down to a steep, rock-strewn slope. They rode hour after hour, Kane thought, and after a while they rounded a mountain top and rode up a narrow path on a ledge on the mountainside. Kane seemed to remember the sound the horse's hooves were making. Yes, there was the plateau!

In the warm sunshine the house seemed large, open and friendly. The grass was a lush green and a stream sparkled across the plateau. Some horses in a corral whinnied to the newcomers. A couple of dogs howled and half a dozen half-breeds ran out to look after the horses.

'Welcome to El Fiero's ranchero, senorita,' Sanderson

smiled. Rita looked at him with unseeing eyes. Kane inhaled deeply and looked around. He saw that there was only one way to or from the 'Eagles' Nest'—the narrow path. And the man who was standing guard on a ledge about a hundred feet above the path could hold off a whole army with his rifle.

Kane realised that he had condemned both himself and Rita. If he had known that the place was so inpenetrable he would never have taken such a hair-raising chance. To come down from the 'Eagles' Nest' alive was an impossibility.

A square, small figure appeared in the doorway.

EL FIERO.

Kane stood with shoulders drooping in the hot sunshine and watched El Fiero come hobbling towards them on his short legs.

'Welcome, Senor Kane,' the horrid little mouth smiled. 'I see that you have brought—er, the goods, and in good condition.' El Fiero chuckled to himself. 'We can assure you that we shall take care of her.'

Four men grabbed Rita and led her into the house. Kane noticed that they were white. One of them was unnaturally pale and his face bore inflamed sores from sunburn.

'Clay,' El Fiero said, his eyes boring into Kane's. 'Our friend is surely thirsty. Have wine placed in my room. This way, Senor Kane.'

The men closed in around them. Kane knew that if he had still worn his revolver he would have drawn it and gone berserk—until they blew him full of holes. He would gladly have died right now if he could take El Fiero with him. But he had no revolver. The hot sunshine struck him and he felt beaten and desperate and his mouth was filled with the bitter taste of defeat.

CHAPTER ELEVEN

Kane sat on his bed in the small room they had put him in and watched the blood-red rays of the sun playing on the wall opposite the barred window. On the table were the remains of his meal and a bottle of wine. A cigarette burned in the ash tray.

He was a guest—and a prisoner.

El Fiero had politely led him into the large room, complimented him on the mission and jokingly remarked about the reaction of his men on seeing Rita's beauty. Then he had raised his glass to Kane, remarked that Don Marco would soon be given the ransom note and that dinner would soon be served.

They had eaten alone in the large dining room, served by mestizos who moved quietly and never spoke. The food and wine was specially chosen and the dinner service was fantastic. It was the first time Kane had drunk from silver goblets and eaten off silver plates. The food and wine brightened him up and after a while he felt safer, more secure.

He nodded to the table.

'Spoils of war?'

'Yes. I accept jewels or works of art just as much as money, Senor Kane.'

'All this wealth,' Kane said, 'to be used up here in the mountains—with no chance of making use of the money?'

El Fiero belched discreetly into his napkin. 'As you have noticed, I am a cripple, senor. Even though I am from a good family—one of Mexico's oldest, in fact, if it is of interest to you—this accident of birth has always cut me off from the surrounding world. Ever since I was a child I have noticed people's contempt, laughter and sympathy, three things that were just as tiring and disgusting to a person who is deformed. I don't miss the world, Senor Kane. Up here I have everything, work, excitement, the best of foods, drink and women, and beautiful objects I can see with pleasure. Remind me to show you my collection of Moorish and Castilian silver work. It is unique.'

Kane sipped his wine.

El Fiero looked at him from across the table.

'You are wondering what is now going to happen to you, Senor Kane?'

'Could be.'

'I haven't decided yet—to be honest. I still need a few answers.'

'About what?'

'To what and who you are.'

'You know that.'

'I'm not sure.' El Fiero's black eyes stared at him. 'You are an unusual man, Senor Kane—not just in looks. Something tells me that you are more than just a gambler and revolvèro that the sheriffs in West Texas drove out of town.'

'What do you mean "more"?'

'You are born to rule,' El Fiero said. 'You are strong, cold and hard. You put money first. You risk your life for money. You have had plenty of time to try your abilities and to show how capable you are. You should have been someone—like I am—and not end up in Mexico as a baby-sitter.'

Kane met his eyes. 'You're right, Senor Fiero. I'm not just the things you mentioned but up to now I've been living in the eastern states. And I did well for myself—maybe not as well as you have, but pretty good. Different things made me leave and it was natural to head west. I decided to take it easy at first so that things could quieten down out east. Don't think that I intend to be a revolvèro for the rest of my life, Senor Fiero.'

'I'm happy to hear it, Senor Kane. I have a lot of good men here in the "Eagles' Nest"—first class men. But they can only obey orders. Working alone and making their own decisions is not for them. Of course, up to now I've only had use for your services. But one day ... in a few years, my activities will have grown to such an extent that I'll need a companero—a partner, as you say in English.'

Kane took another sip of wine. His mind was busy all the time. Did Fiero want him in the gang? Could he hope for a little more freedom—so that he might get a chance to ...

'Don't misunderstand me, Senor Kane.' El Fiero interrupted his thoughts in a horribly precise way. 'You are in no way taken in as a member of the Flagellados and have no possibility of moving around freely ... yet. There is still something about you that I don't understand and that makes me uneasy. If I thought there was any point in torturing you to the borders of insanity to know everything I want to know then I would. But I doubt if there is any point in it. You are too stubborn, too hard. You're the type that would let himself be torn apart, even killed just so that you could stand the thought of living with yourself afterwards. It sounds like a paradox—but you know what I mean?'

Kane nodded.

'You are still my guest,' El Fiero said. 'My house and the whole plateau is yours—but the path is the border. The guard is under orders to kill you if you approach the path. There will always be a guard outside your room now. If this makes you feel like a prisoner then I apologise. Let us say that I ... er ... am protecting you, as a future investment.'

Kane swore and got up from the bed. He went over to the little window and stared out. The sun was about to set behind the Sierra Madre. The valley beneath the plateau was hidden in a mist haze. The shadows were bluish, almost violet.

Would El Fiero check up on him along the Rio Bravo? Would he discover the loop-holes—find out that he was a fake? And would he eventually find out that Kane was a lawman?

He filled his glass and emptied it. He had no idea where Rita was in the house and had no idea how she had been treated. His thoughts settled on rape and he ground his teeth with helplessness.

Somebody knocked at the door. Then the key was turned and a man in white came in. Behind him Kane could make out the silhouette of a girl. For a moment he thought that it was Rita and a wave of warmth ran through him.

'El Fiero sends his greetings and asks if you wish to use this girl, senor,' the mestizo said in broken Spanish.

Kane had to pull himself together and stop gaping. 'No thanks,' he barked. Then with a friendlier tone: 'My greetings to Senor Fiero and my thanks for his kindness but I am much too tired.'

'Bueno, senor. Buenas Noches.'

''noches.'

The door was locked and the key grated in the lock.

Kane went over to the window again. Most likely one of the servant girls he thought, or one of the men's whores. El Fiero certainly looks after his men.

The sun disappeared behind the mountains and it grew dark. Kane lit the oil lamp and sat on the bed again, restlessly. His helplessness and lack of knowledge of what was about to happen was getting him down. He hated to be on the defensive.

He was tired and undressed. Through the window the chill night air drifted in. He crept under the soft blankets. Somewhere in the house he could hear laughter. Footsteps echoed in the corridors. A door slammed, then everything was quiet. Kane listened for a few more minutes then he turned over on his side and slept.

He ate lunch the following day with El Fiero in the large dining room.

'The girl has slept well,' he said, sticking the silk napkin behind his collar. 'She is, of course . . . eh, a little shaken up, but the servants tell me that she ate a good breakfast.'

Kane grunted something in reply.

'And you, Senor Kane?' The almond shaped eyes flickered over him. 'You were very tired yesterday evening?'

Kane said, 'I like to fix up my own women.'

The green film appeared over El Fiero's eyes. The narrow mouth turned pale. 'You can be very irritating, senor,' he said hoarsely. 'Don't bite the hand that feeds you.'

Kane bent over his food. He swallowed the answer that was on the tip of his tongue.

'It perhaps may annoy you to know that Don Marco was informed of the ransom money today,' El Fiero said, his mouth full of fried chicken. He washed the meat down with wine and stared at Kane. "The ransom money wil be three hundred and fifty thousand pesos—in silver, or something of equal value.'

Kane just nodded.

'When the money is safely received in the "Eagles' Nest" then you shall receive your share.'

'Great,' Kane said, wiping his mouth. 'Is it possible to talk with the senorita?'

'No.'

Kane leaned back in the chair while the mestizos removed the dishes and brought in a bowl of fruit. El Fiero greedily took from the bowl but Kane just smoked a cigarette. He wasn't fond of fruit or vegetables.

'There are some things I've been wondering about, Senor Fiero,' he said slowly. 'It's the name of your ... organisation. Flagellados.'

'"The whipped ones" in English,' El Fiero said, stuffing a cactus fruit in his mouth. 'The rumour spread when some of my men, through an accident, were killed some time back. It is very simple, senor—they have been beaten, as their backs could tell.'

Kane nodded to the Sabadilla that hung on the wall by the fireplace.

'That one?'

El Fiero smiled, vaguely. 'Not that one—but one exactly

the same.'

'Is it a form of punishment—or a test of one's manhood?'

'A punishment. But you ask too much, Senor Kane. Won't you try some of these grapes? They are very sweet and juicy.'

'No, thanks.'

El Fiero watched him for some time. 'I thought a great deal about yesterday evening and this morning,' he said slowly. 'I have made a decision. I will let you into some of our secrets with the assurance that the outside world will never hear anything from your mouth!' It was a direct threat and Kane noticed it.

'You mentioned our strange name, Senor Kane—"the whipped ones". We didn't think of that name but it is most suitable. ALL OUR MEMBERS HAVE BEEN WHIPPED!'

Kane's throat was dry. He knew that El Fiero had probably planned to kill him anyway, perhaps because of the previous evening when he criticised Kane's willingness to talk about himself. El Fiero clearly took his doubts about Kane very seriously. It meant that he trusted his instincts, followed them and was willing to pay the price for them later. Revealing the secrets of the organisation now was a sign of the—in his own eyes—genius, explaining to the outsider how clever he really was. Kane had met the same kind of fault before—his thoughts went back to the man that was called Bravado...

'The law in Mexico is considered primitive in the eyes of a gringo,' El Fiero went on. 'Primitive because we don't treat criminals with the same softness like they do in America. It is a paradox, Senor Kane... Your law forbids whipping, for example, but you think nothing of hanging a person—perhaps the most brutal method of execution that is practised. We put a condemned man up against a wall and shoot him! But we also use the whip, if we believe that a whipping will frighten them enough.'

'I doubt if twenty lashes with a Sabadilla is more humane than eight feet of rope,' Kane said.

El Fiero smiled. Grape juice bubbled in the corners of his mouth. He wiped his mouth with his napkin.

'The Sabadilla is not in use today—officially,' he said mildly. 'It is against the law. When one is whipped today, officially, a manilla rope is used, fastened to a wooden handle. It hurts but doesn't tear the skin.'

Kane rolled a cigarette with steady fingers. He waited tensely for a continuation of the story.

'But in Mexico there is a prison, Senor Kane—one of Sonora's state prisons. There the whip is used—by my brother!'

Kane stared at him.

El Fiero dribbled with excitement. 'We recruit men from Casa Fronteras for our organisation. My brother picks out the hardest, toughest, most unscrupulous men there—lifers, the ones that have EVERYTHING to gain. Are you getting the picture now, Senor Kane?'

'You mean—you help them to escape?'

'Exactly! Violent criminals that have avoided the death sentence are beaten with the Sabadilla and put in solitary confinement,' El Fiero went on. 'The only thing they can look forward to is year after year in darkness—until insanity or death frees them. They sit in solitary, Senor Kane—nobody knows that one of them is fetched during the night, nobody knows what happens to him, if he is alive or dead, taken to another prison or set free. My brother shows him the Sabadilla and puts a question to him. We have never had no for an answer! These are men with everything to gain and nothing to lose. We usually reckon on one year in Casa Fronteras—then we can guarantee the prisoner's loyalty.'

'And the authorities, Senor Fiero—aren't they ever suspicious?'

'You are being ridiculous, Senor Kane! Remember, my brother is the prison warden. He writes the death certificates himself—and a cross is placed in the graveyard at Casa Fronteras. Who would ever know that a prisoner is on his way east to Chihuahua? And we never overdo it—we only take the ones we have use for—two a month, maybe three. That is why there are whites, Mexicans and mestizos in the "Eagles' Nest".'

Kane looked at him. There was still something that didn't quite tally. He could see that Fiero wanted him to hear the rest of the story.

'You're intelligent, Senor Kane,' the horrible mouth smiled. 'I see that you are waiting for the rest of the story—the background ... right?'

Kane nodded.

'Exactly fourteen years ago there was an attempted revolution in Mexico,' El Fiero said. 'All the grandes in Mexico agreed to support the revolutionaries, and we gave them money and weapons and equipment. Both my brother and I took part, our money could be used, even though the other grandes would not accept us because of our deformity. You may find this difficult to understand, Senor Kane, but a Mexican aristocrat is more than a landowner—he must be a MAN. He must be able to ride, shoot, seduce women, be an expert with a sabre—in short, be a master at all the masculine traits that have always been a man's fate since time began.'

His eyes looked completely insane now. Kane glanced down at a silver table knife.

'My brother and I are twins,' El Fiero screamed, 'we were born cripples, our legs wouldn't grow. We could never bring attention to ourselves—only scorn and laughter! You understand what that means for a man with proud, Spanish blood in his veins? Do you ... DO YOU?'

The latter came as a bellow.

El Fiero lifted his wine goblet with shaking hands and drank so that some of the wine ran down his chin, staining his cravat.

'The war came, senor ... and we won. The corrupt government in Durango was defeated. But we paid dearly for it, Senor Kane—our father fell in the battle.'

He drank even more wine. His eyes began to be bloodshot.

'Then the victor's laurels were to be shared out,' El Fiero went on. 'The grandes met to find out how the spoils were to be divided out and how much each should have. Mark you, Senor Kane ... neither my brother or I were invited to the meeting! We were worthless ... CLOWNS!'

His enormous shoulder muscles bulged under his jacket. Kane measured the distance over to the knife.

'Oh ... they forgot us completely,' El Fiero said, 'I was offered the title of ALCALDE in a stinking village near our hacienda, my brother offered the position as warden in one of the state prisons. As they said, "positions though of worth are still a poor expression of gratitude to Mexico's brave sons" ...'

'And you and your brother are now getting revenge on these grandes?'

'Right, Senor Kane. For years we wondered how we could do it, retaliate for all the years of ridicule and scorn. Of course we could kill them one after the other, but death is too easy for these men. They can only die once. We found another way ... let them live, but die a little each day, inch by inch. Do you understand? Maybe not—complete ruin means more in Mexico than America. A grande who loses his fortune, his properties and his family jewels is as good as dead, Senor Kane. He is ignored, an outcast, despised, scorned. Just as my brother and I were!'

Kane judged the distance to the nearest knife. He saw how easily it had split one of the cactus fruits that El Fiero had eaten and knew the blade was as sharp as a razor. He chose a spot on the almost invisible throat. The important veins must be around that spot. One quick slash. He couldn't risk stabbing the body. The blade could easily have trouble with those enormous muscles. His right hand moved slowly across the white table cloth. Just as he was about to grab the knife somebody knocked at the door. Kane swallowed an oath and turned. Three mestizos stood there. Between them stood—or hung—a man in bloody clothing.

It was U.S. marshal Ed Zachary.

CHAPTER TWELVE

Kane turned his head and reached for the wine decanter across the table. His thoughts were running wild. Everything had gone to hell! He filled his glass with a steady hand and studied El Fiero's face.

'Who is that?' he barked in Spanish.

'He was found in Encinillas, Senor Fiero,' one of the mestizos answered humbly. 'Someone thought him to be a suspicious person . . .'

Someone, Kane thought, Gonzales, most likely?

'Who is he?'

'We don't know.'

'Chain him to the wall.'

El Fiero turned to Kane as the mestizos dragged Zachary across the floor. Kane didn't even look at him.

'I apologise for this inconvenient interruption, Senor Kane,' he said, 'but you understand that we don't like the traffic around the "Eagles' Nest" to be too large.'

Kane just nodded. He glanced casually at the unconscious figure. It looked as if Zachary had put up quite a struggle. The knuckles on both fists were raw and both the tip of his boots and his spurs were covered with dried blood. Through the ragged clothes Kane could make out ugly bruises and scratches.

El Fiero waited until the chairs were in place, then he barked a quick order and the mestizos disappeared. He got up and went over to Zachary, looked at him carefully for some time, then he raised his head and stared at the face.

'A tough *hombre,*' El Fiero said. 'It'll be interesting to see just how tough he really is. But first . . .' He began to search Zachary methodically. Kane shuddered. Then he realised that nobody else dared do this—it was obviously El Fiero's private pleasure. Kane couldn't see if he found anything as he stood with his back to Kane. A shudder went up Kane's spine.

'Juan!' El Fiero shouted suddenly.

The door was opened. 'Senor?'

'His gun?'

'Here, senor.'

'Put it on the table.'

Kane felt the hair at the back of his neck rise. The revolver that lay on the table was a ·45 Colt 'Police' Special—exactly the same as his own, which was somewhere in the house.

El Fiero hardly looked at the gun and Kane relaxed. He wondered if the revolver was loaded, then saw an opportunity and judged how far it was to the table.

'Come here, Kane.'

He went over to Zachary.

'Take a good look. D'you know him?'

Kane looked at Zachary's bloody face.

'No,' he said lightly.

'All right. We'll make him talk, then.' With two vicious jerks he tored the ragged vest and shirt off Zachary. Kane noticed that the heavily-built mestizo called Juan was still standing by the door. Proof that El Fiero was suspicious about something?

El Fiero fetched the Sabadilla and weighed it in his hand. He looked at Kane. 'Take another look at him.'

Kane did so. He had a sick feeling in his throat.

'Do you know him, Kane?' His voice was no longer polite, but directly threatening.

'No.'

'All right.' El Fiero gave Zachary a couple of savage slaps across the face. His eyes began to focus and clear. They stared over El Fiero's shoulder at Kane. There was no sign of recognition in them.

'What sort of bastard are you?' Zachary said indistinctly, in a superb, drawling, west Texan accent. 'And what in hell's bells is the meaning of this here circus?' The bloodshot eyes were on El Fiero now.

El Fiero hit him again. Zachary's head was knocked to one side. Blood trickled from the corner of his mouth. But his eyes were as hard as flint.

'I'm asking the questions, gringo!' El Fiero screamed. 'What are you called and where are you from?'

'The name's Cuneo. Ernie Cuneo. Say, what the hell...'

Another blow knocked his head in the other direction. When Zachary's eyes were focused again he stared at Kane.

'For crying out loud,' he said hoarsely, 'you're white! What in hell is all this about?'

Another heavy blow. Zachary's lips began to swell terribly.

'Where are you from? What are you doing in Encinillas?'

'Gunned down a guy ... heard about the place,' Zachary mumbled indistinctly. 'Thought I could stay there a while...'

El Fiero took a pace backwards. Out of the corner of his eyes Kane saw three mestizos now standing by the door.

There was open mockery in El Fiero's eyes as he looked at Kane now.

'You two happen to have the same revolver dealer,' he said, pointing with his whip at the revolver on the table. 'I cannot boast of being a revolver expert but at a glance I can see that these weapons you two are carrying are not standard models.'

'It's a new type of Colt that came on the market this spring,' Kane said huskily. 'Thousands have been sold in Texas already.'

'Really? I must remember to tell Clay Sanderson—he's still using his ... obsolete Frontier Colt model 1876.'

El Fiero flicked the whip up and down. 'A strange coincidence, senor,' he said smiling. 'Two hombres—two pistoleros—with the same guns, both in Encinillas at the same time. One or both of you is lying. My theory is that you

Americans are tough enough with a weapon in your hand but without it you're just cry-babies.' He looked at Zachary. 'You will now be introduced to the Sabadilla, my friend. I'll bet you spit out the truth before the tenth lash. And you, Kane, if you know who he is, if he and you are in this together, you must stand here and watch him whipped instead of yourself. Are you aware of this?

Kane said coldly, 'You can tear him apart for all I care, I don't know him from Adam.'

'And you, Cuneo—you don't know Kane, either ... Morgan Kane?'

'If I had he'd never have been able to stand up in this pigpen with any pigs of Mexicans,' Zachary said. 'I'd have given him three hot pieces of lead in the gut!'

El Fiero glanced at one and then the other. Zachary's defiant, bloody face and Kane's hard, unyielding.

He said:

'Go a little to one side, Senor Kane. And I'd advise you to do nothing rash...' A glance towards the door explained what the mestizos' jobs were.

Zachary looked at the whip. He clenched his teeth. Fiero let the whip trail across the floor. Kane wondered how long he could stand watching his friend be whipped. If he cracked he would be signing their death warrants.

He looked into Zachary's eyes. They had a closed look about them. Kane suddenly realised that Zachary was willing to be killed before he'd say anything about their being colleagues. He knew that Zachary was strong enough to do it too. But was he—Kane—strong enough to watch the scene passively?

El Fiero's eyes seemed to glare. The mouth adopted a horrible smile, the muscles swelled in the enormous shoulders—then the right arm swung forward and the whip flashed through the air.

Kane felt the pain physically as the whip tore into Zachary's flesh leaving a bloody weal. Nausea and tension built up inside him and almost impersonally he waited for the moment when something inside him would snap and he would go completely berserk.

The Sabadilla cracked for the third time. Zachary's flesh shook with pain and shock but his eyes still bore the same expression. El Fiero stopped for a moment and looked carefully at Zachary. Without turning he said in Spanish:

'Juan, fetch Sanderson. Quickly!'

'*Si,* patron.'

One less, Kane thought, then saw that Zachary was staring at him over Fiero's shoulder. The gang leader had turned his back on him and was staring mockingly at Kane. Zachary's eyes bore a clear message, and Kane understood what he meant when his colleague looked down at his feet and then looked at El Fiero. There was hardly five feet between them. Could Zachary reach him if he kicked out? And could Kane put Fiero out of action at the moment he stumbled forward? Could he get behind El Fiero and use him as a shield against the mestizos? For they wouldn't dare try to shoot through him.

It was only a matter of seconds now. Zachary didn't wait any longer, this was his last chance!

Just as El Fiero opened his mouth to say something, Zachary threw himself feet first as far as the chains would allow. Both his feet left the ground and smashed into Fiero's shoulders like a ramrod. The air was pushed out of him in an inarticulate bellow and he shot towards Kane like a helpless lump of meat and bones. Kane dodged to one side like a ballet dancer. A shot was fired from the doorway and the bullet disintegrated in the wall beside Zachary. Kane's arm and hand acted like an axe as Fiero flashed past. The blow hacked him across the kidneys. Kane felt a terrible pain up his arm to his shoulder and for a moment he wondered if he had knocked his arm off. El Fiero fell like an ox under the hammer and before he hit the floor Kane was on him again. He landed on his back and in a flash he saw the mestizos almost on top of him; they must have rushed at him as they fired. Kane looked into the two pistol barrels. Fear of the shots that were about to come paralysed him for a fraction of a second. But they didn't come, and he knew that they were afraid to fire because of hitting El Fiero. By then he was in action again. Like a puma he dived at them and smashed them both backwards with two vicious chopping cuts. Two shots roared and showered him with plaster from the ceiling. Kane completely lost control of himself. He only just heard Zachary's roar behind him as he drove four stiffened fingers into the throat of one of the mestizos. The other managed to kick him twice in the stomach and chest before Kane got hold of his right arm. A twist and then a yank and he pulled the arm out of its socket. A revolver lay on the floor. Kane grabbed it and his eyes cleared again. A tall, dark figure stood in the doorway. The shots crashed as one. Kane felt Sanderson's bullet burn a long groove along the upper part of his left arm. But through the smoke of his own revolver he saw the the blood staining Sanderson's white shirt and he gave him two quick bullets which sent him tumbling out of the doorway.

'Morgan!'

Kane whirled around, but not fast enough. Something hard hit him on the head and through a mist he made out the shadow of the Sabadilla and realised that El Fiero had knocked him down with the handle.

Kane got to one knee and raised his revolver but El Fiero was out of the door and it slammed behind him.

Without wasting a second Kane fetched the key from the desk and unlocked Zachary. Kane was still dazed and feeling terrible but Zachary's bloody face and clenched teeth woke him. Kane fetched Zachary's revolver and checked it. It was loaded. He heard two dull thuds behind him. It was Zachary killing the two mestizos. He looked terrible, standing over them with a heavy brass candle-stick in his hand.

'Here, Ed!' Kane threw him the revolver. He helped himself to the two Colt revolvers from the dead mestizos, taking the gunbelts too.

'What now?'

Kane tried to think. 'We'll just have to try and shoot our way out, Ed.'

Zachary laughed and fondled the heavy Colt. 'All right!'

A shot splintered the lock on the door in the middle of the longest wall. Kane kicked it open and dived to one side. A couple of shots whined and the door was splintered. This was routine for the two marshals. Kane threw himself flat and fired while Zachary dodged inside and flattened himself up against the wall. The shots were deafening in the corridor. Two white-clad people fell under the hail of bullets. The marshals ran, grabbed their weapons as they passed and then ran on, sticking the guns in their belts. At the end of the corridor they came to an open hall.

Kane ran in the lead. He noticed the heavy oaken serving table in the middle of the hall. Two long strides brought him into the middle of the hall, then he rolled like a ball the last five or six yards. Bullets spattered around him the whole time, ricochetting from the walls and ceiling. Zachary stood at the end of the corridor with a revolver in each hand firing as if he was on the range. Four shots killed two men who leaned out of open doors to get a good shot at Kane. Then Kane was under cover and fired like mad while Zachary followed suit. Over his shoulder Kane could see the door leading to the open, right outside where they lay. The door was ajar and Kane could see green grass out there.

Zachary felt that Kane was about to dive for the open door and out into the clearing. He grabbed him by the shoulder and shouted loudly,

'Take it easy, Morgan!'

'We've gotta get out!'

'They're waiting for us out there!'

'So what?' Kane was wild with anger.

'We gotta wait a while,' Zachary said, trying to convince Kane. 'I'm expecting them at any moment now!'

Kane shuddered and some of the tension left him. He looked at Zachary's bloody face.

'The Guardia Civil were right on my heels in Encinillas,' he said, quietly. 'They've got the best bloody tracking dogs going. They should be here at any moment!'

Kane looked around the hall. There was nobody in sight,

and no sounds. The dead lay in contorted positions, just as they had fallen.

'How'd you manage it?'

'The police chief in Chihuahua fixed it, plus a pile of warrants that Shane gave me. You weren't the only one who found the cantina in Encinillas suspicious. Every vaquero in the district drops in there now and again. A man with his ears open can pick up a lot there in the evenings, about the haciendas, their owners—and daughters. How'd you come in contact with them?'

Kane listened carefully. He thought he heard a sound somewhere in the house. He answered, absent-mindedly.

'They offered me a stack of cash to kidnap Don Marco's daughter.'

'WHAT?'

'I did it,' Kane said bitterly. 'She's here in the house somewhere.'

'Did you take Don Marco's daughter here?' Zachary was furious, hardly believing what he heard.

'Yeah,' Kane sneered, irritated. 'Now shut your damned mouth, Ed... I think I hear something!'

'No, it's just...' Zachary stopped dead. 'Christ!' he exclaimed. 'Shots!'

Kane got up. 'They've blown the coop! they must have met the boys down in the gully!'

Zachary grabbed Kane's arm. 'Listen!'

They could both hear it. A low, moaning sound.

A woman crying.

Kane's shoulder sank down. Then he noticed for the first time that blood was dripping from his left shoulder.

'She's alive,' he said, hoarsely.

They followed the sound. The whole house was empty. The dead lay where they had fallen. A whiff of gunsmoke drifted through the rooms.

Zachary mumbled: 'The guard out there must have bumped into them down the bottom. They most likely hoped to make a getaway along the Rio Carmen.'

They looked into the room.

Marguerita Marco lay across the bed. Her narrow shoulders shook with sobbing. The furniture was smashed. Kane noticed a bright patch of blood on her shirt. His throat dried up. Zachary rushed across to her. He carefully turned her over and loosened the shirt. Kane leaned against the wall, his arms hanging loosely at his sides. He had seen the bullet hole in the back of the shirt. His eyes filmed over.

'Come here,' Zachary said, quietly.

Kane forced himself to walk over to the bed.

Zachary said, staring him in the face, 'Somebody or other took a pot shot at her. Look here, the bullet...'

For the first time in years, many years, Kane felt sick at the sight of a bullet wound.

He straightened up and stared at the wall.

'Ed,...' he said, huskily. 'Ed.'

'She'll be okay. She must have turned as the shot was fired. The bullet that should have gone right through her just glanced off her shoulder blade and out again through the muscle by the armpit. But she's gonna make it.'

Suddenly the silence was shattered by the tramp of hooves and voices.

Zachary got up. Kane looked down at her. She lay quiet now, a shudder passing through the slight, girlish body occasionally.

'They're here,' Zachary said, his voice sounding strange.

'Get a bandage on her,' Kane said brutally. 'And for God's sake don't play around with her shirt. If the Mexicans see too much of her skin we'll be charged for rape.'

Zachary's eyes were cold. He said slowly:

'You cold-blooded bastard!'

Kane fumbled in his pocket for a cigarette. Zachary repeated, 'You rotten ... oh, to hell with it. Morgan, let's not start fighting now. We'll both hit the roof if we do.'

He raised his arm to put it on Kane's shoulder, but stopped himself. Maybe he felt Kane's repulsion. Kane hated anybody touching him.

CHAPTER THIRTEEN

The horses jogged along in the hot sun. The wind whispered in the grass and small, curled cirrus clouds drifted across the western sky.

Kane and Zachary let the horses decide the pace. They sat with their hats pulled well down over their eyes. Neither of them felt like talking. Minutes became hours.

It had been four days since the Guardia Civil had moved in and burned down the 'Eagles' Nest'. Even the walls had been razed to ground level. It was as if they wanted to wipe the Flagellados and the 'Eagles' Nest' off the face of Mexico's earth and forget the pain and suffering the bandits had brought to the population.

Kane thought of the leader of the Civil Guard. How angry and disbelieving he had been when Kane told him about Casa Fronteras and El Fiero and his twin brother who was warden there. Was it because it had been a gringo that had discovered it? Kane wondered—was it because a Mexican's dishonour had been disclosed? What would happen to El Fiero's brother? Neither Zachary nor Kane were allowed to go there. Because 'the whipped ones' was a Mexican organisation they had no jurisdiction in Mexico.

'An assignment for the Guardia Civil, senores.'

They had been thanked, fed and sent on their way.

'Farvel, senores . . .'

The flies buzzed around them.

Kane's face was dark, locked. They would cross the border the following day. Then a boring train ride from El Paso to Kansas City. The report. Then a trial. What would be his judgement? He could guess. Dismissal—at least.

Kane dropped the thought. He thought of El Fiero. They hadn't found him, either dead or alive. How had he managed to slip away? A secret way down from the 'Eagles' Nest'? Or were a few bribes passed?

He swore inwardly. The whole assignment—the whole business in fact—ended just hanging in the air. No proof. Just polite assurances that everything would be seen to in good time.

Zachary brought him back to earth.

'There's a rider following us. He's going like the devil.'

They stopped their horses and watched the vaquero gallop across the green plain. Even at a distance they could see that he was waving his sombrero and shouting something to them.

He stopped the foam-covered horse and said breathlessly in Spanish.

'Senor Kane, por favor?'

'That's me.'

'I have a letter for you, senor. It is very important.'

Kane glanced at Zachary. Zachary was staring at the horizon. Kane took it, tore open the envelope and read the short latter.

HAVE YOU DECIDED TO GO AWAY WITHOUT SAYING GOODBYE, SENOR? THAT WOULD BE VERY IMPOLITE OF YOU. IF YOUR WIFE (IF YOU ARE MARRIED) IS NOT WAITING FOR YOU, PERHAPS YOU COULD COME TO THE SMALL SHEPHERDS' HUT BY THE MESA VERDE? I WILL EXPECT YOU THIS EVENING, SENOR.

RITA.

'Hm,' Kane said.

He looked at the vaquero's glittering smile under his moustache. 'When did you get this letter?'

'This morning, senor.'

Kane thought about it. 'All right, gracias. Muchas gracias.'

The vaquero smiled again, swung his sombrero and

turned his horse around. He was soon just a speck out on the plain.

Kane stuffed the letter in his pocket. He knew more or less where Mesa Verde and the shepherds' hut was. Four or five hours ride.

'Well?' Zachary said. 'Have they planned a fiesta for you?'

Kane nodded. 'Looks like it.'

'They'll be most insulted if you don't go,' Zachary said, diplomatically.

'I guess so.'

'Anyway I'm not in the best of shapes to meet Shane,' Zachary said, 'a day or two in El Paso will do me good. I'm getting old, I suppose. Need to rest. Can't you pick me up at the Cattlemen's Hotel on the way back?'

Kane felt a pressure in his stomach at the thought of Rita.

'Sure,' he muttered.

'What's she called?'

'Who?'

'Er . . . Trace. Trace Miller.'

'Yeah, that was it. I'll give her your regards.'

Zachary spurred his horse.

Kane sat there and watched him go. With a quiet oath he turned his horse and headed north. He rode as fast as he could. He felt uneasy and excited at the same time.

The sun began to go down. Mesa Verde rose greyish-blue above the plains. Kane rode across the desert-like plain and up the gully towards the summit. On one of his trips he had seen the mesa's lush grass covered by thousands of sheep that grazed there all the summer. He'd also seen the old stone shepherds' hut in a narrow gully, sheltered from the wind and rain during the winter.

When he was almost at the top he turned in the saddle and looked back. Far, far out on the plain he could make out the wood around Don Marco's hacienda. Kane felt the pressure in his stomach again.

He came up on the mesa and headed for the gully. The

shadows were growing deeper. Huge boulders and weathered basalt formed steep walls on each side of the gully.

If Kane hadn't been so engaged in his own thoughts, he would have—or should have—noticed the nervous movement the horse made with its head, as he passed a huge, square rock. He was given only one warning, in the form of a short, whistling whine before something hard and sharp bit him across the side of the head and blinded him for a second.

He instinctively covered both his eyes with his hands.

The tip of a whip!

A SABADILLA!

As the whip was torn away and he tumbled helplessly out of the saddle he heard El Fiero's triumphant roar of laughter. Kane fell heavily, twisted over on to his side and fumbled for his revolver, half blind. A scorching sting across the hand and it hung numb above the revolver butt.

'Up, Senor Kane.'

Kane climbed to his feet. El Fiero stood just a couple of yards away, a revolver in his left hand and the Sabadilla in his right. The evening sun played on the metal and polished handle of the whip.

Kane's brain cleared. At the thought of the letter and his own stupid reaction he was first hot with rage and then cold with shame.

'You love-sick fool,' El Fiero sneered. 'You dribbling, crawling fool of a gringo!'

Kane judged how far it was to him. Right then there was nothing he could do. The revolver was pointing directly at his belt buckle.

'Congratulations,' he said dryly. 'Very cunning, El Fiero.'

'Any fool could trick you, Kane. I've been watching the hacienda—and your movements. It was just a question of time. Do you remember what I said—that nobody leaves Mexico alive with Flagellado blood on their hands.

'Now it's your turn, Kane. This Sabadilla is going to kill you slowly ... bit by bit. Only the buzzards will hear your cries!'

'Let's get started then, you loud-mouthed cripple!' Kane spat, hatefully, hoping for a bullet rather than being killed slowly by the Sabadilla. 'You ain't got a thing to be afraid of, Fiero—I'm unarmed...'

Fiero's eyes glowed red in the sun. His hand shot out and Kane's body shivered as the whip bit through his clothes and into his skin. He sank to the ground and rolled twisting and turning, moaning with pain. El Fiero beat him again and again while his narrow, slash of a mouth spat out oaths and his eyes glittered with insanity. Then Kane saw his chance, his hand gripped the whip, slid a little in the blood before it got a good grip and with his whole weight and every ounce of his strength he pulled. He heard a surprised grunt of surprise and noticed that the whip was suddenly slack. Kane rolled quickly to one side before the shot crashed. He tugged again and El Fiero stumbled forward. Two more shots were fired and Kane was in striking distance. He couldn't feel his wounds now, all he felt was a wild urge to kill, tear, rip apart... His first punch smashed Fiero's nose. His knee flashed upwards, sinking far into the Mexican's crotch. El Fiero screamed like a woman—he dropped his whip and his hands went down to his crotch, while he screamed, his face turned to the blood-red sky. Kane smashed him across the short neck and he heard something snap, then he snatched up the Sabadilla and began to use it. The experiences he had had using a whip along the Santa Fe trail fifteen years previously were suddenly awakened in him. He drove the screaming man across the gully and up the slope on the other side, and then across the flat, hard mesa towards the cliff. El Fiero stumbled, crawled, tried to run—but the whip was there the whole time. His clothes hung in rags, blood lay like black streaks behind him. Then the cliff appeared behind El Fiero. Kane let him stand up, back away and know what was about to happen. El Fiero opened his mouth to scream —those wide-open, insane eyes were full of terror and death —then Kane aimed and cracked the whip for the last time.

He had to shut his eyes when the whip found its mark.

The effect was gruesome. With one final scream El Fiero toppled over ... and then, some time after, a dull roar and the sounds of an avalanche that slowly died away. At last it was quiet, only the wind sighing across the mesa, making a creepy whistling sound in the narrow gully.

'My friend,' Don Marco said, 'words are of so little worth in a situation like this. Let me offer the thanks our government in its exalted position couldn't offer.'

Kane shook Don Marco's hard, small hand.

'You are well again now? No after-effects?'

'A week here at the hacienda can cure anybody,' Kane smiled.

And it was true. When he had dragged himself inside the walls that night a week previously he was in a terrible state, but the treatment the Mexicans gave him put him back on his feet in record time. They had treated him like a prince. He wasn't allowed to do anything except eat and drink, sleep and take a little exercise.

'You're going now?'

'Yes,' Kane said.

A shadow of sorrow crossed the Spaniard's face. Kane saw that he was trying to say something but was having difficulties in saying it. He knew what Don Marco was trying to say so he said quickly, to help him,

'You know how it is ... a man gets a bit home-sick.'

Don Marco looked at him. Kane knew that it was coming now.

'This can be your home, Morgan.'

Kane had to take a deep breath. He knew exactly what the words meant, wealth, a trouble-free life in a beautiful country, peaceful work, ease ... happiness. And Rita.

But he knew that the work at the hacienda would one day be unbearable. He would feel as if he was in a velvet prison. One day he would start nagging at Rita. He knew it. He wasn't made for that kind of life. No false sentimentality, he told himself. You're not sure if you're really in love with her. One day she'll wake from her dream and see you as you really are ... a stranger. We're from different worlds. We'll always be different, worlds apart. One day, when the trouble starts gnawing at me again, will she see it, see through my shadow, into ... what?

He looked into Don Marco's eyes. He saw that the Spaniard knew what was passing through his mind. The slight smile told Kane that he understood Kane and accepted his negative answer.

'You don't need to say anything, Morgan. I hope Rita will forget. I THINK she will forget. Traditions in Mexico are slowly being forgotten, getting freer every day, even an old goat like me is aware of that. Well, mi amigo ... the horse is saddled. Vaya con Dios, amigo!'

'Vaya con Dios, Marco.'

The whole hacienda waved farewell. Kane saw Rita on the balcony. He waved to her. He wondered if she was crying. He hoped not. He didn't see Cathy Taylor. Well, he thought, she's most likely busy correcting essays...

Then he was outside the walls and the sun was warm on his neck. The grass waved in the wind, the smell of cholla in flower, everything filled him with a deep feeling of joy and limitless freedom.

He had hardly ridden two hours when he heard the hammering of hoof beats behind him. He clenched his teeth when he saw the vaquero heading towards him. He thought of the last one, the poor little frightened bastard whom they found drunk and happy in the village, and then explained that he had been given ten pesos by an unknown grande to ride with the letter—without knowing that this grande was El Fiero—the boss of 'the whipped ones'.

Kane felt uneasy as the young man stopped his horse and handed him a note without saying a word, then, turning his horse he rode off again in the same direction.

He read the note:

DID YOU MISS A REAL GOODBYE?
THERE'S A HUT BY SANTA BENEVINUTO.
AND NO SABADILLA ... QUERIDA?

The letter had no signature, but the word 'querida' told Kane what he wanted to know.

He reached the river and small stone hut just before it began to grow dark. The hut was low and lay beneath a huge tree. The smoke from the chimney drifted upwards through the thick branches, and a brown horse grazed peacefully on the river bank.

Kane spurred his horse and rode down to the hut. The sun sank behind the Sierra Madre behind him. The valley lay in deep shadow and darkness closed in.

The horse on the river bank raised its head and whinnied at him.

He dismounted and loosened the saddle. He just let it drop to the ground. His horse ran down to the other. Its head was held high. He went up to the hut. As he placed his foot on the stone step he saw that the light inside was extinguished.

He smiled in the darkness.

'Come in,' a muffled voice said, so quietly that Kane hardly heard it. He took off his hat and went inside. It was dark in there. It had a strange smell, a mixture of woman, warmth and fresh wood smoke. He found difficulties in swallowing.

A slim silhouette appeared. He stood still.

She walked slowly towards him and moved against him.

He kissed her carefully, long, gently. Her mouth was cold to begin with but it got hotter and the rhythm and her heavy breathing excited him. He gripped her by her thick hair and pulled her head back. In the pale light he caught a glimpse of blonde hair.

'Cathy!' he exclaimed.

She laughed, teasingly.

'Disappointed, senor revolvèro?'

'No, but...'

'Didn't you miss me at the hacienda?' Her fingers were hard, searching on his shoulders. Her hips and thighs pressed against him.

'Yeah,' he whispered thickly.

She whispered, 'I won't run any more, Morgan! I remembered what you told me about the marshal who ran away to Mexico to be a cobbler, because nobody shoots cobblers.'

'Aw ... come on, Cathy, I didn't mean it like that...' He didn't like this. Didn't like that she had started a new way of life, had given up a peaceful life—just because of him.

She laughed quietly.

'Don't think I'm going to be a millstone round your neck, Morgan, I've given up my job at the hacienda and packed my things. Tomorrow we can ride off—in different directions—or together—towards the Rio Bravo and the border.'

Tomorrow ... There was a whole night in between and Kane felt her eager fingers in his hair and at the back of his neck.

'All right, Cathy ... we ride together tomorrow.'

She put her arms around him. Her mouth whispered against his, a little troubled, a little soft, a little frightened by the feelings he woke in her.

'Tomorrow, Morgan ... tomorrow. But first this night. Now, Morgan. Now. Now! Now!'

THE END